ALPHA'S BANE

A SHIFTER FIGHT CLUB ROMANCE

RENEE ROSE

LEE SAVINO

ALPHA'S BANE

By Renee Rose and Lee Savino

She ruined my life, got me thrown out of the pack.
The only revenge I crave is her.

Trey

I never thought I'd have a girl like Sheridan. A pack princess—beautiful, smart, one of the elite. She picked me. She gave me her heart, her innocence.

Hurting her was my biggest regret. But then she betrayed us all.

Now she's back—sent to spy on our pack.

She wants revenge.

But my wolf...he just wants her.

Sheridan

He crushed my heart and broke my trust. I ruined his life.

Now we have to work together, and it's killing me.

I want to hate him. But more than that...I want his mark.

CHAPTER ONE

WOLF RIDGE, ARIZONA (NORTHERN
PHOENIX) SIXTEEN YEARS AGO

heridan

THE THUNK of bone hitting flesh knots my stomach. I grab my little sister Ruby's hand and tug her back, out of the way. An inhuman snarl comes from the slender, malnourished teen attacking my cousin Garrett Green, a kid twice his size. You'd have to be insane to take on our alpha's kid.

But Trey probably has a death wish.

His drunk of a dad got hauled in by the police today. For *murder*. Of a human.

And the reason all the kids are gathered on this field behind the clubhouse is because our alpha called a pack meeting. Word is, they're discussing whether to let Trey and his mom stay. The pack doesn't appreciate trouble with humans, especially cops, so any wolf who puts us at risk is subject to banishment.

So yeah, Trey's probably got a world of anger and fear pounding through him now. Taking the beating from Garrett might be a welcome distraction.

To Garrett's credit, he's hardly bloodied Trey yet. He maintains the upper hand but lets the fight go on, lets Trey blow off steam this way, punching and kicking, throwing himself into it again and again. Trey picked the fight as soon as the meeting started and we kids clustered up to watch.

And they aren't friends. No one's befriended Trey since his family moved here last year. He's stony quiet most of the time, barely talks in class, although he seems to be smart. This is the most interaction I've seen from him all year.

It's not as ugly as it sounds. There's a beauty to the fight—both boys moving with light-footed grace, like trained boxers instead of freshmen. If my older brother were out here, he'd break it up, but he just turned eighteen, so he's allowed into meetings now.

Trey throws his weight and tackles Garrett. They tumble to the dirt. Garrett pins him, but Trey slips out and punches him in the temple, eliciting a surprised grunt.

Garrett's four-year-old sister, Sedona, runs forward, crying for him, and I dash in to get her out of the fray. At the same time, Garrett tosses Trey backward, and he knocks me and Sedona to the ground.

A collective growl snarls through Garrett and the group of kids watching. I fully expect Garrett to finish

Trey now, his alpha instinct to protect the females overriding whatever restraint he was showing.

My friend Pam picks up and soothes Sedona.

"Sheridan." Trey ignores Garrett, instantly transforming from out-of-control fury, to... *gentleman.* The wolf in his eyes fades from silver to pale blue.

I didn't know he even knew my name, although why wouldn't he? I certainly know his.

He lifts me to my feet at the same time he scrambles up. His knuckles are bruised and bloodied, but he holds me gently, concern etched in the line between his eyes. "I'm sorry—are you hurt?" His tooth has gone through his lip and blood spills down his chin, but he seems unaffected by his own pain.

Our gazes tangle and something cinches up in my lower belly—some intense new awareness that I'm female, and he's male.

I can't look away. He doesn't release me, even with Garrett breathing down his neck just behind him.

"I'm okay." I finally make my numb lips move. My heart pounds in my ears as I absorb everything I'd missed about this scrappy kid from the lowest pack family. The deepness of his voice. The intensity of his pale blue eyes. The muscle definition on his slender frame. The scents on him—blood, earth and pine.

"Hey." The cluster of kids jumps apart at the command of our alpha's deep voice. "What's going on down here?" My uncle sniffs the air, no doubt picking up the scent of blood. The back door to the clubhouse is open and parents are coming out to round up their kids. Sedona runs to Alpha Green and he tousles her hair without

taking his narrowed gaze off his son. "Were you fighting?"

A muscle in Garrett's jaw ticks as his gaze flicks to Trey, who dropped his hands from me like he received an electrical shock. "Nah." He affects a lazy tone that in no way matches the intensity of the tussle he had. "We were just letting off some steam, right, Trey?" He puts a fist out and Trey bumps it, like they're best buds. Like Trey somehow earned his respect by taking him on.

I release a breath I didn't know I was holding.

Emmett Green turns his commanding gaze on Trey. "You're going to have to man up and take care of your mother now, son."

Trey keeps his eyes dropped submissively to show respect. "Yes, sir. Are we kicked out?"

"No," Mr. Green says. "You'll be permitted to stay, so long as you keep out of trouble and sever all contacts with your dad."

Trey swallows. "No hardship there," he mutters. Then adds, "Thank you, sir."

The alpha walks off and the kids all stay, eyeing Trey with curiosity. I want to punch them all in the face now, even though I am just as much a party to this scene as anyone else. It's Garrett who shifts things up.

"Come on." He smacks Trey's shoulder like they're old friends. "Let's go hang out."

And just like that, Trey gets folded in as one of Garrett's little pack, the bad boy alphas of Wolf Ridge High.

~

Present

SHERIDAN

THOSE WHO DON'T LEARN from the past are doomed to repeat it.

The quote from my 'daily wisdom quote' calendar rolls through my head as I stride across the pitted parking lot. My heels crunch on broken glass and I grit my teeth. I'm here under duress. If I ruin my favorite pair of Jimmy Choos on this fool's errand, I am going to be really pissed.

You can do it, sweetheart. This was just one line from my father's pep talk. *The pack's counting on you,* was another. I hear the unspoken addition: *I'm counting on you.* If there's anything thirty years of life have taught me, it was that I'll do anything to make my dad proud. Including walking back into a scene from my high school days.

Apparently, I didn't learn anything from the past, because here I am, repeating it. Come to think of it, my dad gave me that damn 'daily wisdom quote' calendar.

A rundown warehouse looms across the gravel lot, rising from the cracked concrete. A line of motorcycles lean in front of a broken chain link fence. A few beat up pickup trucks break up the endless row of leather and chrome. I pass one mud-spattered Chevy, a rusty replacement door adding a splash of color to the battered blue. A faded bumper sticker features a howling wolf. Another: a dog with its leg cocked, a telltale arc of liquid splashing on a Ford symbol.

Charming.

As I approach, the door slams open and a shifter staggers out, his matted mane of hair and sweat stained shirt reeking of beer, piss and pot. At 6 p.m. on a Wednesday.

Lovely.

"Excuse me." I'd touch his arm to get his attention, but I don't know where he's been. "Is this the shifter fight club?"

The shifter dude gapes at me, and I stiffen. I'm dressed in an Anne Klein suit and skirt. The olive tone makes the caramel and chestnut highlights in my hair pop and my green eyes look amazing. Paired with the sheerest of sheer stockings and my lucky Jimmy Choos—I'm business up front, yowza in the back. *And sexy as fuck underneath.*

Not that this trifling shifter wolf will ever know it. His gaze roams from my shiny shoes to my elegant skirt to my rather generous hips, detouring around the tailored cut at my waist and stalling right at my girls.

"Hey," I snap. "My eyes are up here."

The shifter looks higher. "Is it a full moon?" he leers. "'Cause I got the urge to mate right now."

A bad pick up line. Awesome.

"No," I bark, no longer willing to waste politeness on this moron. "I'm looking for—"

Behind the shifter, the door swings open, and rock music blasts into the sunny day. A drunken howl fills the air. "Drink, drink, drink, drink!"

Just like that, I'm back in high school.

A keg in the woods, bare-chested shifter boys doing handstands. My heart flutters as I walk up to one. The beautiful troubled one with the ice blue eyes. He turns as I approach, a smile lighting his rugged face. It takes my breath away...

"Lady? Lady..." Beer-soaked breath on my face makes me step back. "I wouldn't go in there if I was you," the wolf informs me solemnly. Great advice. Too bad I can't take it.

"This is Fight Club?" I ask, and when he nods, I hit the door with my palm, sucking in a breath and holding it as I enter the murky underworld.

It takes a second for my eyes to adjust to the gloom. Dust motes hang suspended in the smoky air. To the right, a shifter stands behind a makeshift bar, slinging drinks to his rowdy patrons. A group of leather-clad jackals slam shots. A few sway. One stands on a metal stool, singing a drinking song that sounds vaguely Irish. I can't tell because he's slurring and cussing every other word.

The place is cavernous, with a concrete floor and light sifting in from windows near the ceilings. Whoever converted this warehouse didn't do a bad job. The bar and the backsplash are made of recycled wood. There are a few tall tables, metal topped with more polished wood. Not bad looking, actually. Give this place a good cleaning —maybe a powerwash—and it would look trendy, a hipster brunch spot. Of course, you'd have to change the bathroom signs. Right now they read: *Bitches* and *Studs.*

Enchanting.

I roll my eyes and step aside as a prowl of jaguars brush by, heading to the bar. They have their dark hair slicked back and collars up like wannabe 50s greasers. A few look back at me with casual interest and I fight not to roll my eyes again.

I do not fit in here. For one thing, I'm the only one in a suit. For another, I'm a she-wolf. There aren't many females in this place. A few bitches maybe. Well, I can be a bitch, too. I set my teeth into half smile, half snarl, and stride into the shadows. More shifters stand in clusters, muttering together. One points to a notebook, and his companion pulls out a wallet. Out of the corner of my eye, I see bills change hands. I nearly stop and stare at this blatant proof of gambling.

A large cage sits on an elevated stage. Inside, a scrawny shifter with a shock of orange hair pushes a mop around lazily. My nose pricks with a sharp smell. Blood.

The closer I get to the fighting ring, the stronger the scents hit me. Blood, sweat, piss in a dizzying miasma. If testosterone had a smell, this would be it. I wrinkle my nose and pick my way around the piles of trash, and walk smack into a solid wall of muscle.

"Oh excuse me—"

"Watch it, princess," a rumble like an avalanche comes from a hulking beast of a man. I look up and freeze, mouth falling open. Feral eyes peer from a fight-ravaged face. Arms, neck, cheeks—whatever part of him that isn't tattooed is covered in scars. The scars alone make me stare. With shifter healing, they're not common, but not impossible. How much damage had this guy taken that he didn't heal right away, but scarred?

One beefy hand hovers at my elbow, as if he's ready to grab and steady me—or throw me out. "This is no place for a lady."

"I—uh-I—" This is ridiculous. I'm Sheridan Green of the Wolf Ridge Greens, leaders of the Phoenix pack. Both my uncle and cousin are pack alphas. I've navigated werewolf politics since before I could walk.

I stare up into the scarred face and try to remember my mission and manners. "I beg your pardon."

"You looking for somebody?" he growls.

I straighten my suit jacket, searching for composure. "I...yes. Is Garrett Green here?"

The big guy cocks an eyebrow. "The alpha don't come here."

I lick my lips, trying to think of who to ask for. "I was told this was a pack operation."

"You were told wrong," the big guy tells me. He's a shifter, but I can't scent what type of animal, though I feel it, big and brooding under his intimidating skin. Definitely an apex predator. "This here's independent from the pack."

My brain scrambles. If Garrett's pack isn't running this operation, who is? "I thought this place was under the Tucson pack's protection."

The big guy shrugs. "We're fighters. We protect our own."

"That's"—I shake my head, not wanting to say 'crazy'—"I'm from the Phoenix pack. I was sent here to find out what's going on—"

"Hey, Grizz. Who's your friend?"

I turn towards the silky voice, and get my second shock of the night. Grizz—the big guy at my back, steps between me and the speaker, but not before I get a whiff of cologne. The seductive scent covers an uglier smell—a stone-cold scent like a tomb, with an undertone of old blood.

My lips curl back and I snarl, "Vampire."

The leech is tall, too tall, with a fine-boned face so beautiful it's inhuman. His beauty is predatory, lethal, like a poisonous flower. Men and women will find themselves attracted to him, but before they know why, they'll be dead.

He smiles, showing a pair of pointy teeth. My hackles go up and my wolf surges to the fore.

"Back off, Nero," the big shifter barks, his brawny shoulder inserted between me and the vamp. "She's a guest."

"My dear Grizzly." The vampire spreads his elegant hands. He's wearing a thousand-dollar suit and snakeskin cowboy boots. "Aren't we all?"

"Come on." Grizz herds me toward the back, away from the smiling vampire. "Office's this way. The boss will want to speak with you."

I let the scarred shifter—grizzly bear, of course—guide me around the fight cage toward the corner of the warehouse, where a dark, room-sized cube hugs the walls. Behind us, Nero watches, his teeth shining in the gloom. I suppress a shudder.

"So the rumors are true," I mutter. "This place has gone to the leeches."

Grizz gives me a sharp look and pushes me gently toward the office door. "Someone to see you, boss," he calls and raps the side of the cube.

The door opens and I get my third shock. Spiked hair, lip ring, dark tattoos running up and down muscular arms. And those ice blue eyes piercing me through. I sway as if stabbed, and he automatically puts his hands out to steady me.

Trey Robson.

"Sheridan." It's just like the first time he spoke my name. Trey stares as if he's not sure I'm really here. I'm tall, but he towers over me. And I'm lost, drowning in the past, the heat and memory in his pale blue gaze.

Trey

SHERIDAN GREEN GLARES up at me, looking like she stepped out of my dreams—wet dreams—and into my life. My wolf presses against my skin, clawing to touch her. I don't know whether to yell at her, slam the door in her face, or pull her into the office and reacquaint myself with every inch of her body.

My dick is not so ambivalent. It'd be easy, so easy, too easy, to yank her to me, hike up her skirt, and have her against the wall.

Then she opens her mouth. "Get your hands off me," she spits, her green eyes sparking.

"Fuck," I rasp, and let go of her as if burned. "What's going on?" I ask Grizz without taking my eyes from Sheridan's angry face.

The grizzly shrugs. "She came in looking to talk to Garrett. I figured you'd want to know."

"Garrett?" I cross my arms over my chest, mirroring

Sheridan's stance. She's got her hackles up. As if she has a right to be mad at me after what she did. "Your cousin isn't here."

"I learned that," she snaps. "Right before I ran into a freaking *vampire*."

A growl rises at my chest. Not at her. I'm not happy about the leeches.

"Come in." I step back, holding the office door open. She marches in and turns in a circle, hands on her hips. For a moment I see the office through her eyes. The messy stacks of paper, the dim light broken by the glow of an ancient desktop computer. The empty cans of beer overflowing from the trash can. Not exactly a professional work environment.

Whatever. It's my business and I get shit done when I want, how I want. I'm done trying to please her. Those days are over. She killed any tie we ever had to each other.

A little voice in the back of my head whispers, *You had it coming.* I have to admit, I snuffed out the feelings we had for each other as efficiently as I could. Our relationship was on life support by the time I was through with it. But Sheridan was the one who plunged a knife into my heart, and twisted it until there was nothing left. No love, no feelings. I've been an empty shell ever since.

"Vampire, Robson, really? What the heck is going on?"

Heck. She still doesn't swear. Still the perfect pack princess, working so hard to please everyone. Her family, her pack, her alpha—everybody but me. She doesn't have a problem treating me like dirt.

Right now she's looking down her nose like I'm dogshit on her designer shoe. Her fancy-pants high heels that make her legs under her skirt look long and sexy as fuck.

My eyebrows snap together and I glare right back. Who the fuck wears high heels to an underground fight club?

"What are you doing here, Sheridan?"

A perfectly polished fingernail stabs me in the chest. "You answer me first, wolf. Why is there a leech out there? This is pack territory. Why haven't you thrown him out and staked him as an example?"

"I can't. He belongs to Lucius. We have a deal."

Sheridan sucks in a breath. "You're dealing with vampires?"

"Fuck." I turn away, scrubbing my hand through my hair. I hate leeches more than anyone. They've turned my dream into a nightmare. "It's complicated."

"Explain."

I whirl back on her with a snarl. "I'm not your wolf." I was once. But never again. That's why this is so hard. "I don't answer to you."

She straightens, her chin going up in the stubborn stance I know so well. "I'm here on behalf of the Phoenix pack."

"Garrett's dad? You should talk to Garrett."

"I thought he'd be here."

"This isn't pack territory. Not anymore." I swallow to stop my wolf growling in my chest. He hates the leeches as much as I do. "We made a deal with the new kingpin."

"I can't believe this. The wolves I know would never ever deal with vampires—"

"The Sheridan I knew would never choose her own glory over her friends. Oh wait, she did."

She pales. "That was years ago," she whispers. "I thought you'd be over it."

Never. I'll never be over you. If I talk, I'll beg like a dog. For her to come back, forgive me, anything. Instead of answering, I raise a mocking eyebrow. Cruel, but she deserves it.

She looks away, color returning to her cheeks with a flush. A tendril of hair curls around the perfect shell of her ear. I tighten my hand into a fist to keep from touching it.

After a minute, Sheridan turns back, her face a cool mask. "I'm here representing the Phoenix pack. We've heard Fight Club was attracting trouble. Alpha Green sent me to figure out what's going on."

"Spy on us, you mean." I cock my head and bare my teeth in a nasty semblance of a grin. "Just like old times."

She flinches at that. Points to me. "I'd like a sit down with Garrett, to talk about this new vampire presence and what it means."

"Then call him. I'm sure your cousin will be happy to hear from you. Or are you not on speaking terms with him?"

She presses her lips together and gives a small shake of her head.

"Imagine that. It's almost like no one trusts you anymore, since you betrayed us."

"Are you ever going to let that go?"

"Nope." I grin to hide the flash of pain. She's so beautiful. So perfect. So out of reach. An ant has a better chance of dating the sun.

Her father was right. I never should've put my dirty paws on her.

"Look." Her voice softens. "I'm not the bad guy here. Fight Club"—she flicks her fingers at the door—"You're attracting attention. Cops, FBI, CIA—"

"Whoa, whoa, whoa." I raise a hand to stop her, mentally cursing Agent Dune and his damn midlife crisis. "That business with the CIA wasn't us."

She shakes her head. "You were involved. And now the heat's on and you're taunting the humans under their noses. Gambling. Illegal fights. Drugs."

"Hey"—I spread my hands—"I have nothing to do with drugs."

She leans forward and sniffs my clothes pointedly. "Last time I checked, recreational pot wasn't legal."

I roll my eyes. "Maybe I have a prescription."

"I don't care about the pot. I care about the harder stuff. *Sucre sang.*" She rattles off something French-sounding. "Sugar blood. It's a new drug on the streets, and it's deadly." She pauses, her eyes faraway for a moment. "That's why the vampires are here," she says to herself, as if she's just figured it out.

I stay quiet, drinking in the sight of her in a sleek suit. She looks good. More makeup than she used to wear, and her hair is pulled back tight, but the stuffy suit she's wearing doesn't hide her perfect curves.

Sheridan. Fuck. She's catnip to my wolf. Not catnip— wolfbane. Sweetness and poison in one perfectly made up package.

15

As if to prove it, she faces me. "This little turf war with the leeches makes it clear that you guys can't stand alone. You need our protection. Maybe even become part of the Phoenix pack again."

"What the fuck?" I can't keep my voice down. "We've been on our own for years, ever since you—"

"You only exist because we allow it," she says, cool as a judge pronouncing an execution sentence. "Shut Fight Club down, Trey. Or I will."

CHAPTER TWO

TWELVE YEARS AGO

SHE-WOLVES IN BIKINIS, empty beer bottles, sand between my toes. San Clemente State Park is the perfect place to camp with the gang on an October weekend.

My mom's easy, but I'm not sure how most of these kids got their parents to let them come—must be because Garrett, our future alpha, headed up the trip. Either that, or they lied and said it was a school outing.

I know if I was Sheridan Green's dad, I would never let her sleep anywhere near the likes of us. Of me. Because she is in serious danger of getting marked right here and now.

And it's not just the stolen beer keg talking.

We've never hung out before—we run in totally different circles, but somehow we ended up playing frisbee in the water together this afternoon. Now she leans against me in front of the small beach fire someone lit, the skin of her bare shoulder warm against mine, her scent in my nostrils. I haven't touched her yet, mostly because I don't trust myself. I can't even believe we're hanging out. Homecoming queen, pack royalty, straight A student—she's everything I'm not. At seventeen, she works in the upper offices of Wolf Ridge with the rest of the royalty, not on the factory floor, like me and my mom.

And she's the most *gorgeous* she-wolf this pack has ever seen.

I thought she'd date an alpha kid from another pack, someone like her cousin Garrett, who is and has everything. Or even Jared, who at least has a mid-pack pedigree.

"You know what I can't figure out, Robson?" Her voice is husky and soft so only I can hear her.

"What's that, sweetheart?" I take a hit off the joint Jared passed me and offer it to her. She shakes her head, but I don't sense judgment.

"Why a guy as smart as you sits in the back and screws around during class. If you applied yourself, you could get a full ride to college somewhere."

My chest tightens but I force a laugh. I wrote off college a long time ago. Probably about the time my eighth grade teacher told me I was as worthless as my imprisoned dad, and I should get my ass into vocational school. "What makes you think I'm smart?"

"You wouldn't be in the advanced classes if you hadn't tested in. And you ace every test even though I never see you study."

She's been paying attention.

That in itself makes my world shudder and rearrange.

"Nah, school's not for me. I can't stand authority." I flash her my bad boy smile and she leans into me, her forest green eyes lit by the flames.

"You follow *his* authority." She lifts her chin in the direction of Garrett Green, our pack leader's son.

"He's different." I mean it. Garrett may be one-hundred percent alpha, but he's one of us. He doesn't care for school or authority, either. He won't toe the party line. He's told his dad point blank he will never run the brewery. More than anything, though, he's a friend. He's as loyal to his mini pack of teen wolves as we are to him. He'd do anything for us.

And I've had way too little of that in my life, so yeah—I'm sticking close. Where he goes, I follow. And we sure as hell aren't going to college to become suits at Wolf Ridge Brewery.

She turns her gaze back to the fire.

Across the way, Garrett howls and strips off his swim trunks. With a whoop of excitement, the rest of the boys follow, dropping their suits and shifting to howl. A bunch of girls, do, too, calling to me and Sheridan. She stands up and hesitates, shooting an unsure glance at me.

As much as I'd give my left nut to see Sheridan Green naked, there's no fucking way I'm going to let her do it front of the rest of the gang. Yeah, we've all been shifting together since we were kids, but that was before puberty. Before our teeth bore the serum capable of permanently marking a female.

"Not here, sweetheart." I snatch her up by the waist

and run, carrying her toward the cluster of tents while she giggles and fights me to put her down.

I drop her in front of her tent and turn my back. "Last one on four legs is a rotten egg!" I shove down my trunks and shift while she's still ducking into the tent.

She squeals in frustration and then darts out, her tawny coat thick and shining. She runs at top speed down to the water and I chase, nipping her heels, my wolf already ready to mate, to mark.

Down, boy. Sheridan Green is about as far off limits as a nun in the Vatican.

My wolf doesn't give a shit.

He wants her. Preferably in human form, naked and on the beach.

He wants her tonight.

Present

SHERIDAN

FOR A SECOND TREY just stares at me, eyes wide as if I shot him in the chest.

Again.

The pain and shame of that night comes back to me like a black fog rolling over my body. I've tried so hard these last twelve years to claw free from it, to believe I did the right thing. Especially since the Tucson pack has done well for itself.

My first boyfriend then turns and kicks the leg of the desk.

"Fuck," he spits. "Fuck fuck fuck." He kicks a trash can and it goes flying.

"Lovely," I drawl, stopping a rolling beer can with my foot. "You always were so eloquent."

"You were never this much of a bitch," he shoots back, and I flinch.

"I can't believe I ever loved you," I mutter. I don't mean him to hear but he glances up sharply, anger flushing up his neck. Stupid sensitive wolf hearing.

I raise my chin, daring him to comment.

"What the fuck is this, Sheridan?" There was a time I would melt when he said my name. Very inconvenient to remember that right now. Trey is angry. Very angry. But the wolf in me feels his heat and interprets it differently. She remembers when Trey's big body and all his anger at the world became fiery passion he unleashed on me. The perfect alchemy.

"You show up after twelve years, talking big… let me explain something, sweetheart." He jabs a finger in my direction. "You don't have the authority to shut me down."

"My alpha does."

"So you're going to turn tail and run to him? You were always good at tattling on us. Twelve years hasn't changed a damn thing."

I flush. Score one for the angry he-wolf.

"That's not why you're here." Trey crowds me, giving me an eyeful of the flexing muscles of his chest, and suddenly I can't think straight. "I think you got tired of your pretty little place in the pack and pretty little life. Is that right, sweetheart?" The shaded edges of his neck tattoo fill my vision. It's hot, almost too hot to breathe. "You always wanted to walk on the wild side. That's why we were together in the first place. I wanted to get my dirty paws on a pack princess, and you"—his breath warms my ear and I feel dizzy—"you were slummin'."

He steps back to survey my dazed expression, a satisfied look on his face. My blood rushes faster, faster, and my wolf wants to know why we still have so many clothes on.

"That's why you're here." Trey folds his arms over his broad chest, effectively closing himself off. "Another taste of the dog's life. Then it's back to your cushy gig, after you piss all over everything I've done. Because you're still out for revenge."

"This isn't personal."

"The fuck it isn't." He tosses his beautiful head, and I recognize the flash of pain beneath the fighter's stance. It's the very thing that attracted me to him when we were teens—what gave him depth. He wasn't another dumb meathead follower of Garrett's. His emotions ran deep, and though he kept them bottled up most of the time, they came out through his fists, and with me, through passion.

I just want to move close and comfort him. As angry as he is, I know he won't hurt me. He would never hurt me.

"You still have it out for me."

"I don't." I swallow, trying to wet my mouth. I need to remember why I'm here. I need to remember that Trey is a player, and any attraction I feel for his beautiful fighter's body will soon be obliterated because deep down he's a lying, cheating low-down dirty dog. "I represent the pack."

"Not my pack."

I want to scream at him, ask why he's playing stupid. "The Phoenix pack. Wolf Ridge. Your old pack."

"That never was my pack." His lips barely move.

"Please," I scoff. "Tell your mom that. She misses you, by the way. Still works in the factory—I see her every week."

His eyes narrow. "I talk to her twice a week."

Okay, maybe that was a low blow, insinuating that he abandoned his mom.

"You know, I'm surprised your father lets you descend from on high to mingle with the commoners." He prowls around me, and I fight the urge to turn, face him, keep from giving him my back. He's the biggest predator in the room and my wolf knows it. She shouldn't be so aroused. A little more arousal in my scent and Trey and anyone who walks in this room will know how I really feel. My wolf wants to climb him like a tall, tattooed tree.

Down girl!

"I'm not a pack princess."

"Could've fooled me. What did they make you when you graduated college? CEO?"

"I'm a VP of Finance." I cross my arms over my chest. "But I earned it."

Trey scoffs.

"No really, I did. I interned every summer. By the time I graduated with my MBA, I had worked in every area of the company."

"Every area?" Despite himself, he sounds impressed.

"Yep. Factory floor, janitor. I even did a summer in marketing at our sponsored and outdoor events. When we were short on staff, I helped out wherever—waitressing, even behind the bar."

"You slung drinks." Treys' voice is dry, disbelieving.

"Yep. "

"Good, we need a bartender who can make change. Wednesday night, 7 p.m. Wear a skirt." He sneers at my outfit. "But lose the jacket."

"Aren't you listening? You can't run fights here anymore. You're attracting attention."

"Then you're not paying attention, sweetheart." Trey crowds me, and heat fills my body. I stare up at him. Every nerve's clanging like a fire alarm. *Evacuate now!* "There's no way in hell I'm going to let you shut me down."

He leans forward, eyes on mine. Angling his head, he takes a good long sniff. "Vanilla and orange," he purrs in his deep voice, and arousal pools between my legs. "Very nice."

"It's the flavor of our new line of seasonal brews," I parrot my company's marketing spiel. "Wheat beers. Very popular." My brain is on autopilot, all available neurons diverted to keeping me from grabbing Trey's bulging biceps with both hands, and rubbing against him like a cat.

"Whatever it is, I like it. You smell good enough to eat." His eyes are glinting silver, his wolf peering out at me. Not good.

I slam my heel down on his foot. Hard enough to send my pointy heel through the thick boot leather.

"Ow," he shouts, jumping back. "What the hell?"

"Darn it," I hiss, lifting my leg. My heel is broken. I point to his boots. "Are those steel toes?"

"Factory regulation." His lip curls again. God, is he ever going to look at me with anything but contempt? "You know us Robsons. No sense wasting a college education on us. We work the floor."

"Stop it," I snap, no longer upset about my shoe. I hate it when he implies he's not smart enough. "You have a brain, Trey. I told you that years ago. You just choose not to use it." I hike up my skirt and prop my foot on the desk, baring my leg right in front of him.

"What are you doing?" Trey chokes out.

A tendril of satisfaction snakes up my throat. I may have lost a heel, but I'm regaining my footing. "Taking off my shoes." I slide my fingers up my thigh to unsnap my garters. "But first, I have to take off my stockings. Don't want them to get dirty."

Trey's Adam's apple bobs as he swallows. He licks his lips, staring at my legs. "You can't go out there in bare feet."

"I'm a tough she-wolf," I shoot back, skimming the stocking down my calf. I may take a second or two longer than absolutely necessary, but the stunned look on Trey's face is worth it. "Watch me."

Trey

25

FOR A SECOND, I do. I watch the show, and fates help me, I love it. Sheridan's slim fingers peel down the stocking, revealing a perfect leg. She removes one, then the other, balls them up and stuffs them into the toe of the broken shoe, straightening to shoot me a triumphant glance. "If you're not willing to discuss things like a reasonable person, this conversation is over." Barefoot, she pivots to leave. No fucking way is she walking barefoot across the club—my club—the floor covered in broken glass and dirt and fuck knows what.

Hips swaying, she takes one step out the door.

"Not so fast." I grab her around the waist and hoist her easily over my shoulder. She struggles, shouting, legs kicking helplessly as I secure her in a fireman's hold.

"What the heck," she squawks, but I'm already moving, striding through club, past startled shifters. A few turn and point, hands slapping over their mouths at the sight of me carrying a struggling skirt from my office. Out of the corner of my eye, I see Grizz. The huge bear shifter shakes his head.

"Trey! Put me down right now or so help me—"

"Keep screaming, sweetheart." I laugh, freeing my right hand to give her sweet ass a smack. "Make sure no one in the place misses the show."

"I'm going to kill you!" Sheridan bellows, her fists beating my back. She's strong, but I'm stronger.

"You can try. We'll call it an audition. We're thinking of getting some more women fighters in. Maybe have 'em mud wrestle, naked. I'd pay to see that."

"You, you—" her voice disintegrates into a growl as she digs her nails into my ass. The sting shoots straight to my dick. Goddamn Sheridan, causing me pain, my dick just loves her more. She could cut me off at the knees, and I'd still fucking cum.

"That's it, baby, take a chunk outta me. I like it rough," I mutter as I hit the door and step into the night. Sheridan growls, but she stops struggling so hard. I enjoy the last few strides across the parking lot. I head past a gang of curious bikers straight to Sheridan's car. The white Mercedes convertible that her dad got her as a graduation present. A perfect gift for his perfect little angel.

I drop her right into the front seat, as gently as I can, before backing away quickly. Don't want to get my dick punched. "Where are you staying?" I have to ask—nothing will stop the need in me to take care of her—make sure she's safe.

She looks up at me, hair tousled and cheeks flushed and eyes glowing with rage and...something more. "I rented an Airbnb on Meyer Street. Over by the convention center."

I can't focus on her words because the scent of her arousal hits me and I trip backwards. Oh fates. She's turned on.

"Well, check out of it, sweetheart," I tell her. "Don't come back."

She drives out in a spray of gravel. I stand, unflinching, as the stones shower my jeans. The sting is nothing I don't deserve.

"Trey." A tall dark shape emerges from the murky shadows around the bikes. My best friend, Jared, prowls forward, his forehead wrinkled in disbelief. He hooks a thumb in the direction of the retreating Mercedes. "Was that…"

"Yup," I answer and turn on my heel to stalk back into the club. I don't want to talk about it.

Sheridan Green. Fuck.

CHAPTER THREE

TWELVE YEARS AGO

"I HEARD you've been hanging out with the Robson boy." My mom brings this up casually over dinner, knowing full well it's going to get my dad's attention.

He stops chewing his steak and puts his fork down. "Pardon me?"

I roll my eyes and shove a forkful of steak in my mouth. "I hang out with a lot of kids." Not a lie, but it *is* a pretty cowardly response. Trey means more to me than other wolves. And we're not just hanging out—he's my boyfriend.

My friends don't get it. Trey isn't alpha material. His mom is basically omega of this pack, and she's lucky our alpha even let her stay in Wolf Ridge after her drunk of a husband caused all kinds of trouble with the human police.

But I know the truth. Trey may look like a rebel with his pierced lip and multitude of tattoos. He may seem like a thug because he's quick to jump into fights with his buddy Jared, but he's not a punk. He's quiet. And, I've learned, thoughtful. And super smart. *Still waters run deep.*

Definitely underappreciated.

Maybe I have a penchant for fixing broken things. Maybe I'm just fascinated by the pull of his soulful blue eyes, the ones always watching me. The ones that turn silver under the moonlight.

Or maybe there's just no explaining the attraction— our wolves like each other and we're just following along for the ride.

Either way, I know Trey's the one.

The guy I'm going to give my V-card to.

"I don't want you spending time with him or kids like him," my father pronounces, reaching for the bowl of steaming baked potatoes and serving himself two more.

"Why's that?" My voice comes out colder than I mean it to, which is a mistake.

My dad looks up sharply, reading into it, knowing what it infers. "Because they're trouble, and you know it. Those kids aren't going to college. They aren't going anywhere. And they're way beneath you."

"You think every wolf's beneath me, Dad."

"Because most are. And you should be focused on college right now. Keeping your grades up and your nose clean."

I make a show out of looking around the dining room

in bewilderment. My little sister, Ruby, snickers. "Have my grades slipped? Am I ever in trouble?"

My dad presses his lips together.

"No," I answer for him. "My GPA is 4.2, I'm still in the honor society, Varsity math team, editor of the yearbook and—"

"I know," my dad cuts in. "I just don't want you to lose your focus. Not when you're so close." My parents have a lot riding on my success. My brother used to take the brunt of their ambition. Now it's all heaped on me.

I glance at my mom for help, but she shakes her head. She doesn't like the idea of me hanging with Trey either. Both my parents would prefer to see me with the prince of a neighboring pack instead. A royal match.

"It's my senior year of high school. I've already aced the SATs. My college apps are turned in. I think I'm allowed a little fun. You can't tell me you two didn't at least try to enjoy your youth before it was over?" They've told me enough stories about their high school romance for me to know they had plenty of fun.

My mom glances at my dad from under her lashes and blushes, and I get that sappy sweet warmth in my chest I always do when I see how much they love each other.

"Well, I still don't want you dating the Robson boy," my dad grumbles.

This time I can't betray Trey by denying our relationship. "I think it's time you trusted me and my own judgment. I'm practically an adult."

My dad sighs, but I can see I've won—for the moment. "I'm counting on you being responsible."

I flash a saucy grin. "When am I not?"

Present

Sheridan

I'M STILL BREATHING HARD when I pull into the driveway of the casita I found through Airbnb for this fun little Tucson sojourn. By *fun* I mean anything but. I must've been crazy to have volunteered for this job.

Tis better to have loved and lost, than never loved at all...

"Yeah right," I mutter. Whoever compiles the stupid quote calendar should just try it then: loving hard and getting your heart ripped out. Bypass surgery without anesthesia.

Hell hath no fury like a woman scorned... That's more like it.

My cell rings just as I'm barreling up the front walk, barefoot, broken heels in hand.

"Hello?" I answer, my mind still whirling from the night's events. Trey Freaking Robson. Still hot. Still handsome. And annoying as heck. *How dare he throw me over his shoulder like...like...like a 'little woman'! Who the heck does he think he is?*

"Sheridan?" My dad's voice breaks through the angry haze. "Are you there?"

"Hi, Dad. yes, I'm here."

"How's Tucson?"

Words cannot express. "It's fine." I juggle the phone as I dig out my keys. "I went to Fight Club today. Garrett wasn't there but I talked to one of his guys." *Shouted at him is more like it.*

"Good, good." My dad sounds a bit distracted. "Emmett is making some calls on his end, but I went ahead and booked two months of the casita. Just in case."

The first key I shove into the lock fails. I grapple to find another, and drop one of my shoes. "Thanks, Dad. You didn't have to do that. I do have my own money. I was a VP, you know."

"Still are a VP," my dad says firmly. "I told the board you just needed a break. That the pack needed someone to handle this Tucson mess, and you were the one they trusted."

"Yeah." I try another key and it jams. *For Fate's sake.* At this rate I'll be sleeping on the doorstep.

"You'll get everything there straightened out, and be back before you know it. The department isn't the same without you. Just don't take too long." His voice takes on the hokey singsong that tells me he's about to make a joke. "I need you back here so I can retire."

"Ha ha." I pretend laugh. In forty years as CFO, my father hasn't deviated from his daily schedule. The same desk, the same meetings, the same daily wisdom quote calendar. The day he retires is the day wolves fly.

I fit another key into the lock. It slides in easily, but the knob won't turn. With a sigh I set down my purse. Before I turn back to the door, a prickle of warning runs up my spine. I turn to the road.

A sleek black vehicle with tinted windows turns into the cul-de-sac, rolling slowly past. I can't see who's driving. At the end of the drive, it seems to pause, and my hackles go up.

"One more thing and I'll let you go." My father's tone turns businesslike. "We don't know what exactly's going on with Garrett's pack, but there are rumors vampires have moved into Tucson. Not one of the friendlies, but an older one who wants to set up a new base of power. If he claims pack territory, it could lead to war. Watch your back."

"I will," I whisper. Without a sound, the mystery car starts moving again, and creeps on down the road.

Finally, finally the knob turns when I twist the key to the right. I wrench the door open and enter the stale-smelling rental, stooping to pick up my broken shoe and my purse, nearly dropping the phone.

"Take care. We're counting on you." We exchange goodbyes and I lurch into the house, letting everything I'm holding clatter to the floor. I shut the door and flick the deadbolt, my mind scurrying like a mouse. Who was in that black car?

I pick up my phone from the floor, scrolling through my contacts instinctively. Who should I call? Alpha Green has bigger things to deal with. Besides, he expects me to complete this task on my own. That's why he chose me.

Call Trey. I delete the thought as soon as it comes. I haven't called Trey since we were in high school. I probably don't even have his number.

But when I type in his last name, I do. *Robson, Trey.* I remember his twitch whenever I called him by his last name tonight. He hated it. I loved that I can still affect him. If he doesn't love me, I'll take his hate.

My finger hovers over the familiar number. Now that I see it, I remember—I knew it by heart. There was a day when he was the first person I spoke to in the morning, the last voice in my ear at night. But I haven't leaned on Trey in a long, long time.

Get out of here, sweetheart. Don't come back.

I hold the phone in my hand and clench it hard enough to hear the plastic crack.

Never, never, never give up.

I'm not eighteen, innocent and vulnerable and ready prey for a guy like Trey. It's not like he can break my heart. Not again.

This time, he won't get rid of me so easily.

CHAPTER FOUR

TWELVE YEARS AGO

ALPHA GREEN, himself, picks us up from the police station after letting us spend the night in jail. Not juvey, either. All of us are eighteen, so we went to County.

Emmett Green is huge, imposing, like Garrett. The guy never fucking smiles, but right now he looks ready to commit murder.

"Possession of marijuana." His voice drips with condemnation. It's pack law to stay out of trouble with human authorities, so his own son getting picked up must rub him raw.

"Someone has it in for us—" Garrett starts to say, but his dad barks, "Not a word."

Garrett's right. Someone tipped the cops off. They specifically showed up at school to search the three of us.

It had to be someone close to us, someone who knew where each of us kept our stashes—me under the seat of my motorcycle, Jared in his jacket pocket; Garrett in his car.

Someone wanted to get us in trouble.

Alpha Green honors his own request for quiet, giving us the coldest fucking silent treatment the entire ride home.

No—not home. He drives straight to the pack clubhouse. Garrett, Jared and I exchange glances as an icy realization slithers down my spine.

They called a meeting.

About us.

This isn't fucking good.

We go in, and it's just as I feared. Every adult in the pack sits waiting for us. A stony silence falls when we walk in.

A grinding sound starts up in my ears. I recognize it—it's the one that used to play when my dad beat on my mom. When the cops came and took him away. When the pack kids whispered behind their hands about me and the adults met to discuss whether they should let my mom and me stay.

My face feels hot, fingers and tongue go numb.

We're called up, one by one, and questioned. I don't even know what's said. I answer truthfully, mechanically. There's no strategy, no thinking. I've already gone into life-is-over mode.

We sit while the pack deliberates.

It's not until Lance Green, Sheridan's dad, gets up to rail against us, saying we must be made an example of, and we're a danger to the younger wolves that it all falls in place.

You'll regret this.

Sheridan.

Would she be angry enough to do something like this? Call the cops on us and have us arrested?

From the satisfied look Mr. Green sends me, I'm fairly certain she did.

Our alpha doesn't seem happy about it, but he throws in his vote against us, and just like that—we're banned from the pack.

Not permanently—a four-year ban after which we can request re-evaluation of our status.

Garrett's hands close into fists and he stands and stalks out.

Jared and I follow, accompanied by the sound of my mother's broken sobs.

Present

Sheridan

WEDNESDAY NIGHT, I pull into Fight Club's ratty gravel lot, park, and jump out like I've hit an eject button. My door slams so hard, I check it for dents. A crowd of bikers turns and stares. I ignore them as I stride across the broken concrete, focusing on the club door. It's either that or flip them the bird.

I'm horn-gry. Horny and angry, and tired from tossing and turning all night with my nethers throbbing. I refused to rub one out, on principle. I am not going to lie in bed and touch myself while imagining Trey Robson and all the things we say. I am *not*.

No! My boot connects with a chunk of pavement, and when I kick it with more force than necessary, it flies off and almost takes out one of the wannabe greasers.

"Watch it, sister," he barks, patting his hands over his perfectly slicked back hair as if checking for damage.

I bare my teeth at him. His gaze sweeps down and up my corseted form and he forgets to obsess over his coiffure. Appreciation lights his dark eyes, and his lips start to form a whistle.

"Don't do it," I snap, and he blanches. My Lily Munster makeup must be super scary. "If I wanted to be hooted at like a pinup girl passing a construction site," I inform him gently, "I'd have taken off my jacket." Then, lest men complain that I'm never nice to them, I peel out of the butter-soft leather, revealing the tight green-and-black satin corset underneath. It's Scarlett O'Hara tight and does wonders for my boobs. Not that the girls need any help.

I spin on my heel and strut away to a chorus of cheers.

By the time I get to the club door, I feel marginally better. Without slowing, I put out both hands and shove, hoping some bodies fly on the other side. They're shifters; they can handle it. *Sheridan in the house, bitches. And studs.*

As I slam my second door of the night, everybody in the dark space turns. I stand with hands on my hips, a queen surveying my new kingdom, giving everyone a chance to take me in.

I've outdone myself with my outfit. I'm in a corset dress with a tiny tulle skirt, which showcases my fantastic bust and hips and hugs my waist. The lace of my stockings tops my knee-length New Rock boots. More punk than biker chick, but it works. I brought them with me on a wild hair, thinking that this trip away from my dad and pack might give me more chances to party. The boots are perfect for the fight club—steel-toed and satisfyingly heavy. No way am I breaking another heel in this pit.

I head straight to the bar, and everyone shifts out of my way. A harried-looking young man rushes around behind the polished wood, tossing my jacket onto a shelf beneath the counter. Without a word, I head to the sink and start washing glasses.

A few minutes later, the rushed bartender appears at my elbow. He's dark and slender and smells faintly of fur. Jaguar, if I'm not mistaken. "Hey, I'm Luka. Can you pour?"

"Nice to meet you, Luka. Yep, I'm here to help."

"Thank the fates. William Wolf, neat. Cheetah at the end of the bar." He points out the whiskey bottle and the customer before rushing off.

I grab a clean glass and the correct bottle, and strut to my first customer, a burly biker-type. His eyes fasten on my upthrust breasts and he stills. I smile. I smell a good tip.

My eyes settle on a tall, tall guy a few feet behind him, and my smile widens. Grizz the grizzly bouncer stares at me, then shakes his head and turns away, rubbing his head like it pains him. He doesn't come over and throw me right out. Good sign. My plan is working: get in, get behind the bar, and get people to talk about the leeches and their potential drug dealing.

So far, so good.

"You worked here long?" my customer asks, still staring at my chest. He looks a bit dazed. I tilt the bottle and let whiskey flow, leaning forward a little to give him a better view. I'm not about to let my best assets go to waste.

Then I see him. Standing next to Grizz, chin down, eyes ice, face frozen. Trey Robson watching me flirt with a club patron, and he can do nothing about it.

My night just got better.

"Just started, actually," I say. "Am I doing a good job?" I shrug my shoulders and his eyes follow the movement of my breasts. I knew this corset was a great idea.

"Uh, huh," the Cheetah murmurs. "I think I'm in love."

"Mmmhmmm," I murmur noncommittally. A wave of scent hits me, like the first wave of rain, hard and potent. I'd recognize this scent anywhere.

Trey storms towards me, thunder in his expression and lightning in his eyes. He's filled out since high school. Now he's massive as a mountain and beautiful as a god, and every molecule within me quivers as he closes in.

"What do you think you're doing?"

"Slinging drinks." I pretend to be unaffected by him, even though every hair on my arms stands up, electrified in his presence. Bowing my head, I putter around and search for a cocktail napkin.

"We need more napkins," I tell Luka as he rushes past.

Meanwhile, Trey looks like he's about to explode and rain fire down on the premises.

Excellent.

"You said you needed a bartender." I polish a few glasses briskly, my smile turning cool.

"I was just showing her the ropes—" Luka offers, and falters when Trey turns on him with a stormy expression.

"Office. Now," Trey orders me. His big hand closes on my arm, but I shake it off, giving a thumbs up to poor Luka as I head to the back.

As soon as I'm inside, Trey gets in my face. "What the fuck are you doing back here? I tell you to leave and you show up to serve drinks?"

"Can't beat 'em, join 'em." I shrug. Yes, it's a calendar quote.

"I know you're spying on us."

"Yep. Like my disguise?" I prop my hands on my hips and do a Wonder Woman pose that shows off my girls. Trey's eyes nearly bug out of his head. Poor guy, he's never seen me like this. After we broke it off, I had to let my wild side out somewhere. Can't do much under my dad's nose, but once in awhile, I like to dress up and party, and when I dress up, I do it right. Sexy clothes, crazy makeup, outrageous shoes—like Halloween. I run around looking like a slutty extra from *The Rocky Horror Picture Show*, howl at the moon, and stuff it all back down into a suit when I head to the office on Monday.

"No," he lies. The hunger in his eyes says otherwise. "Sheridan, what the fuck are you wearing?"

"This?" I fiddle with the satin ribbon set neatly

between my breasts. "Just something I had on hand. Should be good for tips."

His eyes fix on my fingers a moment. "You can't wear that," he rasps. He drags his eyes away, rubbing the back of his neck with a big, tattooed hand. His fingers twitch. I wish he would touch me.

"You told me to wear a skirt," I say in a saccharine voice. I know it's stupid, but I press closer to him. The peaks of my breasts are dying for stimulation, but when I brush against his hard chest, it only amplifies need through the rest of my body.

Trey's eyes flare but he doesn't back up. His head drops so his lips are an inch from mine as he growls, "If you're bartending, I'm your boss."

"Oh and you have a dress code?" I give the piles of papers on his desk a scathing look.

Trey rears back, shoulders shrugging as he removes his jacket. His arms come around me and he tucks me into the heavy leather. "We do now."

I open my mouth to make a smart-aleck comment about 'dress code' and 'discrimination' and 'HR', but I can't talk about company policies when his lips are close, so very close to mine.

His jacket is still warm from his skin. Not about to mention I left my own jacket behind the bar, I pull his tighter around me and shiver. The world falls away until it's just me and Trey in this black box. No space, no time, just a heady scent rising between us and his dick prodding my belly. *Yes, please.*

Then he clears his throat and takes a step back.

What? No!

"Thanks for helping out. Luka's wanted us to hire help since the night crowd picked up." He walks to to the door and holds it open without meeting my eyes. "I'll let you get back to it."

I'm frozen, too shocked to even glare at him. I strut in here like a goth's wet dream and he's just gonna...pass?

Not that I expected him to pull me in here, strip off my naughty outfit, and fuck me against the wall. I did not want that. No way. I learned the hard way that Trey's a player.

I stand there, biting my lip, and after a few seconds I realize I'm staring at his belt. Specifically, several inches below it. Several looooong inches.

"Fuck," Trey growls, and stomps off, leaving me even more horn-gry.

So. Very. Horn-gry.

∼

Trey

I STEP straight into the walk-in cooler. Maybe it will chill me the fuck out. Seriously, I am not going to make it through this night. Sheridan Green dressed like a Playboy bunny hopping around Fight Club?

My wolf is growling.

He wanted me to claim her back in high school, and I never did. Every damn time we had sex he wanted to mark her. But we were just kids, and she had a bright, shiny future waiting for her. I wasn't about to saddle her with my sorry ass before she even graduated high school.

Probably the only reason I didn't go moon mad was because I was still growing. My hormones weren't those of a fully grown male yet. I didn't reach this height and size until long after she left for Stanford.

Long after she got us thrown out of the pack.

I have a full-on boner from our interaction back there, but my chest's tight, too.

Being this close to her, seeing how her wolf still responds to mine—it makes the loss of her so fresh. She was beautiful as a teenager and she's a fucking knockout now. Like a thirteen on a scale of ten.

I pop the top off a beer—yes, it is a Wolf Ridge pale ale —with my teeth and guzzle half of it down.

Jared walks in and stops when he sees me, then leans a broad shoulder against the walk-in door and chuckles. "You gonna survive this?"

"Fuck, no," I spit out.

He jerks a thumb toward the club. "Did you hire her?"

I chug the rest of the beer and wipe my mouth with the back of my hand. "I was kidding! I didn't think she'd take me up on it. I also told her to get the fuck out and never come back, but she didn't take that part seriously, did she? Fuck."

Jared's expression grows serious. "What's she doing here?"

I meet his eye. "You know."

"Spy?"

I nod. Emmett Green has been sending spies since the day he threw us out on our asses. Hell, Garrett's second,

Tank, was originally a spy sent by Alpha Green. He didn't think we'd survive on our own. Big packs brainwash you to believe that—shifters have to stick together or they won't survive—that kind of bullshit.

The Wolf Ridge pack never imagined we'd land on our feet. But all the young pups left with us—they'd follow Garrett to hell and back. After the charges were reduced to misdemeanors, we moved to Tucson. Garrett got us work flipping houses. We put in sweat equity and started making money fast. Once Alpha Green saw we were a success, he ponied up investment capital. Now Garrett owns half the real estate downtown. Take that Wolf Ridge brew-fucks.

"She's got her eye on Fight Club?"

"Says she can shut me down."

"What a bi—" Jared swallows the rest of the word when he sees my expression.

Even after everything, I never let them talk shit about her. In fact, she became an untouchable subject around me.

She may have ruined our lives, but I know her actions were born of pain. I ruined her first. She was only fighting back the one way she could.

And while part of me is still pissed off that she didn't know me better—didn't keep believing that I'd never willingly hurt her—I know that's bullshit. I made damn sure she'd walk away from me and never look back.

So I guess we're probably even. Or at least I thought we were.

But her showing up here and throwing her weight

around—squeezing her body into that depraved fucking outfit?

I have to question her motive. Is she looking for revenge? Or does she just want to rub my nose in what I missed? Because I sure as hell don't get the peace and reconciliation vibe from her. Unless this is foreplay to her and she's hoping we can wipe the slate clean with an epic fuck session.

Well, if so, I'm in. My wolf's been in since the moment she breezed into town.

I toss the empty beer bottle into a recycle bin and walk past Jared. He thumps me on the back. "Stay strong, man."

Yeah, right.

Resisting Sheridan's an impossibility. At this point, it's just a matter of how soon I get her pinned beneath me. And whether this time she'll escape my mark.

CHAPTER FIVE

TWELVE YEARS AGO

I HAVEN'T SEEN Trey all week, which is beyond strange. He's never given me any reason to feel insecure about him. About us.

In fact, since that night on the beach when I made the first move and plunked down beside him at the fire, all his focus has been on me. That doesn't mean he doesn't hang with his buddies, Garrett and Jared, but that's usually if I'm too busy.

This week, though, he's been working on motorcycles and hanging out at Garrett's every day after school. He told me he wouldn't be able to give me a ride home today when I ate with him at lunch, and he's been distracted and quiet—not that he was ever Mr. Talkative.

It's Friday night and I text him after dinner. A bunch

of kids are going up on the mesa to drink and hang out. It's the usual weekend scene and if he and I don't do something just the two of us, we often meet there.

Me: *You heading to the mesa?*

Trey: *Nah, I have some shit to do.*

My stomach knots because I sense the lie straight through the screen. He's never lied to me before. Never been anything but up front. Why would he? Does this have something to do with selling dope for Garrett? Maybe they're in trouble. I've never liked that Garrett, Jared and Trey are the pot dealers for Wolf Ridge and the nearby 'burbs like Cave Creek and Scottsdale. It's sort of that thing we've tacitly agreed not to speak of.

Yes, they are wolves, which means human dealers and potheads would have a hard time hurting them, but a bullet to the head would still kill a wolf. And they're not above the law, either.

And with Trey's history—after what his dad did—he'd be out of the pack in the blink of an eye if the cops ever pulled him in for anything at all.

Because I'm not one to just roll over, I call him on it.

Me: *Why don't you tell me what's really up?*

Trey: …

He doesn't answer for five minutes. Then:

Trey: *Meet me at our table.*

I know what table he means. The picnic table where we first made love. I grab my purse and head out, my heart thudding. I imagine all kinds of bad scenarios— Trey's already been caught by the cops and no one knows, they're being hunted by a dealer, someone's hurt.

I drive straight to our picnic table and find Trey

already there. He's looking over the side of the mountain toward the city. The sunset casts pink and orange hues over the earth, reflects off the Saguaro needles, making them glow.

Trey doesn't turn around, which shoots another spike of fear through my chest.

I walk to stand beside him. "What's up?"

"Hey." He doesn't turn to look at me.

Goosebumps stand up on my arms. What in the hell could be so wrong?

"Trey, *what's going on?*" I demand.

His throat bobs in a swallow. "I think we should see other people."

Air comes out of my lungs in a choked laugh. Not that I think he's joking. Not at all. It's just so far from what I expected that my body chooses the wrong reaction.

"What are you talking about?" My voice cracks. I ball my hands up because they're shaking so hard I don't know what to do with them. I want to punch him, to push him down the hill. To make him take it back.

"Yeah. You're leaving at the end of the summer, so I just figure we should cut our losses early. I'm ready to play the field again."

"Play the field?" My brain can hardly compute his words—they are so out of character. Trey never was a play the field kind of guy to begin with. This makes no sense.

"Are you trying to make sure I go to Stanford?" I croak.

He turns, finally looking at me, and I swear I see nothing but pure agony in his gaze, but just like that, it disappears and his expression hardens. He shrugs. "You're going. I'm seeing other people. That's how this works."

I stumble back.

This isn't Trey talking.

Not the Trey I know.

Trey would never be so callous, so cruel.

"It's for the best, Sheridan."

I shove him. "Just tell me what this is about, Trey. *Tell me.*"

Pain flickers over his expression. His lips tighten before he opens them to speak. "I'm letting you go." He flips his keys around his finger and walks to his motorcycle.

I run at him, shove him from behind. "You're fucking everything up!" Tears choke my voice, spill hot down my cheek.

He bows his head, barely turning his face toward me. "I know." His voice is so quiet, a human ear wouldn't hear the words. Before I can answer, he's on the bike and moving, away from me.

Away from us.

Away from everything I thought had meaning.

Present

Sheridan

"You okay?" Luka asks.

I set down the bottle with exaggerated gentleness even though I want to yell and scream and cry. It's amateur night at the club, and a bunch of biker cats surround the cage, yelling for or at one of their friends. Trey's nowhere to be seen. Since our meeting in the office, he's avoided me.

And even though I've spent the night peering into dark corners, looking for evidence of vampire/drug activity, I've seen nothing. Not even a flash of fang. I'm busting my hump pouring drinks and laughing at lame pickup lines, and I won't even have something to report to my pack. I need a t-shirt: *I visited Shifter Fight Club and all I got was beer spilled on my corset dress.*

"Fine." I smile a little when he pours me a shot. Luka's not a bad shifter bartender—a job that requires finesse and speed and a sense of shifter politics, particularly when dealing with drunken, fight-ready big cat bikers. But he really can't make change. He's desperate to keep me.

I usually don't drink on the job, but tonight's kicked me in the teeth, and this isn't my real job. I lift the glass to my lips and savor the burn.

Then I see who's standing at the bar and almost choke.

Nero, the leech, leans on the polished wood, silky blond hair falling in his face. "Hello again."

I slam the shot glass down, not worrying about whether it will break. I'm a she-wolf, and I feel safer showing strength.

"What's your poison?" I ask. "We don't have a ton of arsenic back here, but for you…"

"So impolite." The vamp shows his teeth. I stare at a point

on his forehead, feigning boredom. Even I know not to look a leech in the eye. "And here I was going to give you a big tip."

"Save it," I mutter and start to turn away.

He pulls out a few bills and waves them in my direction. All of them Benjamins. Why would a vamp carry so much cash? He's in a nicely tailored suit and looks like he just came from a job downtown where the plaque on his office door reads 'Analyst,' but I doubt he got that stack shorting stocks. Is he here to deal?

I stop to ponder this, and he smirks, thinking he caught my attention with some green. "Hennessy Paradis."

I fight the urge to laugh. Who comes to a rundown shifter club and orders cognac? Only a vampire.

Instead I hand him a bottle of Wolf Ridge. A new IPA my company is calling 'Luna-tic.'

Nero grimaces like I've given him a bag of dung.

"Try it," I say sweetly. "I'd garnish it, but we're fresh out of garlic." I don't wait to see if he does try it. I don't care. Everything is wrong about this place. Vampires are hanging out in a shifter bar like they own the place, and Trey doesn't seem to care.

I grab a rag and swipe the bar, and a strong, cool hand grasps my wrist. I snarl, catching the stoney scent of the vampire.

"Be still," he hisses, a seductive tone that chills me. Vampires can control people with their gaze. But some of the old ones only need to use their voice.

"Let go of me," I growl and he does, but stays close, his manicured fingernails drumming on the bar.

"I need to give you your tip, little wolf."

I want to grab a bottle and smash it against the bar, and use the shards to cut off a vampire's head. But something's up, and I need to find out what.

He pulls out a hundred dollar bill and folds it in half. I swear to the fates, if he tries to tuck it between my breasts, I will clock the guy. "Are you coming to the territory meeting tonight?" he murmurs.

I go still. "What territory meeting?"

"We invited the wolves out for a discussion. Midnight. Santa Cruz wash, south of Congress."

I raise my head and look at the clock on the wall. It's almost eleven.

Nero drops the C-note on the bar, puts a finger to his lips and glides away, leaving me cold.

"You all right?" Luka asks for the second time.

"Yeah." I try to shake off the eerie chill running through my limbs. There is nothing natural about a vampire. "How long have the leeches been coming around?"

"Since the beginning. There are a few in town who run No Return, a nightclub on Congress." The shifter shrugs. "They're all right. But this is a new crowd. Lucius Frangelico, an old vampire king, moved outta Hollywood, starting over. They do that, you know, every fifty years. So people don't realize they don't age."

"Yeah. But what's he doing here?" I whisper the question to myself, watching Nero's back as the tall vampire heads deeper into the club. He ignores the fight, going straight to a side door, opening it and disappearing.

Luka picks up the bottle he left, and drops it into the

recycle barrel, glass clinking against glass. The sound jerks me out of my trance.

"Here." Luka hands me the hundred-dollar bill Nero left. "You earned it."

At ten to midnight, I rinse my hands and slip away, telling Luka I need a break. I thread through the groups of shifters standing around talking about the last fight, and when I reach the side door Nero took, I hesitate only a second before pushing through it. I don't know what's going on with the leeches in what should be wolf territory, but if Trey and my cousin won't talk to me, Nero might. If not, maybe he can lead me to this Lucius Frangelico vampire king. Once I find out, I can report back to my Alpha and my dad, and go home. Before history repeats itself with Trey.

The night air is cool on my face as I walk. It's easy, way too easy to follow the vampire's scent.

Trey

MOONLIGHT POOLS IN THE ARROYO, lining the ruts thirsty for water. There's no sound but the highway in the distance and the crunch of our boots on the dry rock.

"How much farther?" Jared asks, just as a large shadow detaches from a group of rocks and flows down into the empty basin.

"There." Tank, the pack's second in command, jerks his chin towards the shadow, which cleaves into several distinct bodies. My skin prickles as I recognize the new arrivals. Dark and suit clad, with slick hair and inhuman good looks. Vampires.

My lips curl automatically, showing my teeth.

Garrett waves us forward. He marches right up to the group of vampires, stopping a few feet away from their leader. Tank, Jared and I fan out behind him, acting cool and unafraid. A few more of our pack take up watch positions in case the leeches decide to ambush us. So far they've acted in good faith, but I don't trust them as far as I can throw them. I'm not sure how far I can throw a vampire, but it sounds like a great way to relieve stress.

"Alpha," the vampire leader greets Garrett. The kingpin, as we call him, is lean like a runner, with swarthy skin and an impeccably tailored suit. His name is Lucius Frangelico and he looks like he should have some corny Transylvanian accent. Instead, he speaks in cultured tones, like a BBC newscaster. "What a fine night you chose for our meeting."

Behind Frangelico, the rest of the vampires stare at us like snakes, unblinking. They're all perfectly groomed and wearing dark suits, mirror images of their boss. They look like fucking yuppies who stepped out of the office to get a cold brew, but their scent tells me they're old. We're not sure how old, but between me and a few of my hacker friends, we've traced properties their leader has held for over two hundred years. The shell corporation changes every few decades, but everything ties back to Frangelico.

"Glad you all could make it," Garrett answers blandly.

Lucius tilts his head to the side. It's a natural movement, but I get the feeling it's one he's studied and copied.

He waves a hand at his gang. "These are my lieutenants, Maximus, Nero, Tiberius and Augustus."

"The Roman Empire called," I mutter to Jared. "They want their emperors back." My best friend chuckles silently, his shoulders shaking.

In front of us, Garrett hooks his thumbs in his jeans and lets his chin drop. On any other wolf it would be a submissive pose, but our Alpha is so big, he's still looking down on all but the tallest of the leeches.

"That's a lot of mouths to feed," he says thoughtfully, and Jared and I stop joking.

"That is why we meet, no?" Lucius spreads his large hands. He's pretty big for a leech. Most of them are pretty boy thin and—forgive me—anemic. "To work out territory."

"Tucson's not big enough for all of us, plus your gang."

"We prefer the word *nest*," Nero corrects. At a hand signal from Frangelico, he comes forward, offering a sheet of paper. "Here is a map of the area. We have marked out ample territory for the wolves, with access to all the mountain ranges, of course. We merely wish to dwell west of the Santa Cruz, and south of Congress Street. To hunt and feed in peace."

At Garrett's signal, I move forward and meet the sleek-looking vampire halfway, keeping my gaze somewhere between his ear and his shoulder. Without touching his fingers, I grab the map and hand it to Tank.

He and Garrett study it a moment, and when Garrett looks up, his eyes glow with anger. "See, we have a problem with this. Because you don't hunt and feed off rabbits or deer. You hunt humans."

Moonlight glints off Lucius' fangs. "My children are too well-trained to make a mess of our food."

"I've heard otherwise. I heard you got into a turf war in L.A., and your victims ended up drained dry."

"A small issue only." Frangelico waves a hand. "Here I have no enemies. I offer you much to continue the good-will between our species."

"What exactly are you offering?" Tank asks, folding beefy arms over his chest.

"The continued survival of your pack," Lucius replies, and the temperature plunges twenty degrees.

"What makes you think you'd survive a fight with our pack?" Garrett asks.

"You are young. You have only begun to take mates. You have too much to lose." Lucius' voice is matter-of-fact as he recites his reasons. He's pretty nonchalant for a guy who just threatened our entire existence.

And our mates.

But he's right. Our strongest pack members—Garrett, Jared and Tank—all have mates they would do anything to protect. And she's not my mate, but fuck if the image of Sheridan in her goddamn corset-dress doesn't materialize in my mind, making my fingers clench into fists. I would die to keep her safe without a moment's thought.

Loud growls grow in several wolves' chests. Garrett snaps the map in his hand, and the pack falls silent.

"It says here you'll be claiming Phoenix for your feeding grounds." Garrett studies the paper in his hands. "Have you spoken to the pack there? I doubt they'll be happy to know a new vampire nest is trespassing on their territory."

"They won't." A clear voice drifts down the side of the ravine, and we all turn. Sheridan appears at the top of the hill, swinging a leg over the concrete barrier and making her way down, crunching rocks under her big boots.

"Who is this?" Frangelico asks sharply.

"She's one of us," I blurt and lean close to Garrett and Tank to let them know, "It's Sheridan."

"What the fuck?" Garrett's forehead creases, but he motions for Jared and me to go to her. We meet her halfway up the side of the ravine.

"Hello, again," she says calmly, as if she's not interrupted a tension-filled meeting between sworn enemies. She's still wearing my jacket, thank the fates. The whole goth makeup and corset getup makes her look like a depraved Tinkerbell.

"Hi." I grit my teeth and put a hand out to help keep her from sliding down the loose rocks. She smells like beer and the vanilla-orange scent of her perfume. My favorite scents in the world. My dick perks right up.

I'm still mad as hell. "What in the fuck are you doing here?"

"My job," she chirps, and strides forward to meet the vampires.

The leeches wait with perfect poker faces, honed over hundreds of years. Lucius moves first, stepping forward with a little bow. "I do not believe we have been introduced."

"I'm Sheridan Green," she says, walking right up to stand beside Garrett as if she's his equal. As if she belongs here. "I represent the Phoenix pack."

"My lieutenants reported no Phoenix pack," Lucius tilts his head at Sheridan, questioning.

"Wolf Ridge," Garrett answers for her. "It's north of Scottsdale. My father's the Alpha."

"Ah yes, Alpha Green. I have heard of his rule and the little schism between him and his son. You are the son?"

"As if you don't know," Jared mutters, and I resist the urge to roll my eyes. This whole playing dumb act of Lucius' is getting old. He's trying to be disarming. But we know all about vampire charm. Let it get to you and you're dead. Sucker food.

I move closer to Sheridan.

"I am," Garrett answers. "But, as you can see, there is no divide between me and my father's pack. We are united on all fronts." His voice holds a warning. *Attack one and you'll have to fight us all.* Score one for our alpha.

"I see," Lucius says pleasantly. "It is well that a Phoenix representative is here. The proposed territory allows my children to feed there as well as here. We can spread out our prey."

"Spread out the deaths, you mean," Tank rumbles.

Lucius makes an impatient gesture. "No deaths. And with the opening of our club, we may not have to roam too far."

"Club? What club?" Sheridan asks. I lay a warning hand on her back, but she doesn't back down. I sense her tension, but she faces the vampires with a calm, almost bored expression.

"My new club, Toxic," Frangelico tilts his head towards Sheridan. "You must visit us, my lady."

"No fucking way," I mutter, and step in front of Sheridan, putting as much of my body between her and the vampire king as he'll allow.

Lucius keeps smiling at Sheridan, showing fangs. She smiles right back, her incisors front and center. Her creature-of-the-night outfit has one advantage to it: the hot dress and artful makeup is one hell of a costume. Combined with her smarts, she charms the vampires completely. Too well. Out of the corner of my eye, I watch Nero lick his fangs. I bite back a growl.

A crackle of paper and we all snap back to attention. Garrett holds up the map.

"For purposes of a temporary treaty, we agree to this territory," he says. "Any vampire caught outside will be subject to punishment."

"If any of mine are caught breaking my rules, I will deal with them myself," Lucius promises. His voice is smooth, almost a purr. The leech is pleased.

I feel sick. I didn't glance at the map, but I bet the fight club is right inside the vamp's territory. Which means we might have to pay tribute or be overrun by leeches hunting their victims. Not that we haven't been already. Garrett wouldn't let us throw any vampires out until we met with Frangelico.

"Wait," Sheridan says. "What about *sucre sang*?"

There's a silence as wolves and vampires alike try to make sense of what she said. It sounds vaguely French.

"What is this?" Lucius sounds surprised.

I hear Sheridan's heartbeat pick up as all eyes turn to her, but her chin lifts and her voice stays strong. "I've heard of it in connection with leeches, I mean, vampires. Some sort of drug, right?"

A few of the lieutenants exchange knowing looks. Nero hides his mouth behind a manicured hand.

"Ahh," Lucius says. "Sweetblood. I had not heard the street name. It is not a drug. Well, not for humans, anyway."

"Not directly," Nero murmurs.

"It is for vampires only." Lucius spreads his hands and looks smug. "You come to our club and I will show you. All of you are welcome, anytime."

A low growl from Garrett makes the vampire king add, "No harm would come to you or yours. You would be our esteemed guests."

"All right," Sheridan says. At first I can't believe my ears—she's calling the vampire's bluff? Lucius inclines his head and Sheridan adds, "I'll go. Saturday night." Then she glances up at me and the look on her face...it's a challenge.

The scraping sound is me gritting my teeth, biting back my response before I say something I regret and set off a war. I can't stop myself from glaring at Nero when he glides forward and leans towards Sheridan. "You will enjoy yourself, little wolf. I will make sure of it."

"This meeting's over," Garrett growls, thank the fates, and one by one the wolves turn and walk back the way we came. I wait for Sheridan to go, and glare in Nero's general direction before spinning on my boot. The leech's laughter starts as soon as I turn my back, unhinges my spine and follows me from the ravine.

Up at the cars, Sheridan is surrounded by the pack, talking to Garrett. I can't stop myself from marching up and grabbing her arm. "What the hell were you thinking?"

"Back off, biker boy," she spits back, wrenching her

arm from my grip. Shit, I forget how strong she is. "You're not the boss of me."

I ignore her, turning to Garrett. "She's not safe here. My bouncer told me one of the leeches—Nero—took an interest in her. You gotta send her back to Phoenix."

"I'm right here, moonhead," Sheridan snaps. It's her turn to grab my arm and jerk me to face her. "I am perfectly fine. I can fight my own battles."

"The fuck you can," I growl and talk over her head to Garrett. "Did you hear her? She's going to go into the leeches territory—to their club!"

"I heard," Tank says. "I think it's a good idea."

"What?" I whirl on him. I swear I'm going to sock somebody in the jaw. My wolf writhes under my skin, ready to wreck someone.

"Hear him out," Garrett orders.

"We know Frangelico is powerful, right? But we don't know much about him. We need to know more. Visiting the nightclub is the perfect way to find out more."

"Then why don't you go?" I shoot back.

Tank shakes his head. "Can't. I'm too high up in the pack. Also, I'm a threat." He shrugs his massive shoulders. "We need someone less thug-like. More professional."

"A spy," Garrett agrees, and turns to Sheridan. She flushes but doesn't drop her gaze. "What do you say, Cuz? You're already here to keep tabs on us."

"It's not like that," she protests weakly, and for the first time since she's shown up, she looks uncertain. "I'm not here to spy on you."

"Uh huh." Garrett raises a brow. "At least do me the favor of telling the truth."

She drops her eyes. "They're worried, and not just about the leeches in our territory. Your pack has been through a lot." Sheridan sucks the inside of her cheek. It has the unfortunate resemblance to sucking dick, and my cock stiffens to full mast. I almost groan out loud as I shift it in my jeans.

"I know. I'll call my dad." Garrett grimaces for a brief moment before smoothing his expression. The rest of us share sympathetic looks. We all know what Alpha Green can be like. After all, we grew up under his rule. Until he kicked us out.

The way some of the pack eyes Sheridan, they haven't forgotten the part she played in betraying us. Under the weight of the pack's stare, Sheridan wilts a little. She was one of us, before she turned traitor. "About tonight...I was just trying to help."

"Help who?" His voice is whip sharp.

Even though I agree with Garrett, my wolf bristles at the way he's speaking to her. My chest puffs out on its own, shoulders square. Garrett glances at me and takes in my shift of posture.

"Help you." The waver in Sheridan's voice bothers me far more than it should. I step closer to her, make it known I'm still her protector, even after the way things went down.

Garrett shrugs. "I know you have to follow your alpha's orders. Maybe you can be useful to both of us." His voice turns thoughtful, and I don't like the look in my alpha's eye. "What was it you said about the drugs the vampires are dealing? Sugar blood?"

"I only have rumors your dad told me about. Bodies

have been turning up around the seedier parts of Phoenix. Drug addicts who OD'd on bad product—that's what the humans think. Whatever drug it is, it makes the victim's blood toxic. Too much and they die."

"That's not enough to get my dad involved," Garrett rumbles. "He's not interested in a human war on drugs."

"No," Sheridan agrees. "The reason Alpha Green is worried is because the bodies have been tampered with. Fang marks. Signs of use...by vampires."

Everyone in the pack sucks in a breath.

"You think Frangelico is behind this?" Tank asks, his eyes narrowed as he puts two and two together. "His vampires are feeding too much, too often, and dumping the bodies, making it look like a drug overdose?"

"That's correct." Sheridan nods. "That's why I came here. We're listening closely to the human authorities to make sure we catch these deaths early. In case we have to intervene."

"Intervene," Tank repeats. "You mean cover up."

Sheridan raises her chin. "If we have to. The more suspicious the deaths, the more the humans will go poking around into the existence of paranormals."

"Dangerous for all of us," Garrett says. "So that's why you're looking into Fight Club?"

"No." Sheridan's voice is dry. "Fight Club is a problem in and of itself. It's all over the human police and FBI channels. Alpha Green isn't happy about that, at all. The club seemed a good place for me to start investigating. Then I met the leech and realized the vampire drug trade and the club might be intertwined."

"We're clean," I put in. "I don't allow trade on premises."

"You know as well as I there's no way of monitoring that, not one hundred percent," Garrett says. "And even if you do catch one vampire at it, you can't do more than kick him out. You'd have to bring him to Lucius for discipline, or risk offending the nest."

I grit my teeth because it's true.

"If it helps," Sheridan pipes up, "I think the vampires aren't messing around with shifters. Just humans they can lure in as victims. I think the club might be cleaner than one run by humans."

Tension in my gut loosens at Sheridan's defense of the fight club, and not just because I want to save my club. Having her speak up on my behalf means something to me. Too damn much. I need to cut this cord that binds us so tightly, even after all these years.

"One more thing," Sheridan adds. "I'm here to investigate, and keep my pack safe, but I don't want to cover up the deaths. I know we have to hide evidence of paranormal tampering on any bodies we find, but I'm not here to do the vampires' dirty work. I'm here to stop them."

My stomach plummets. Sheridan's got that look in her eye, the one that says she's planted her flag and will stand by it at all costs. I know that look. The last time, I was the one she chose to stand by. It cost me everything to get her to change her mind. We barely survived the fallout.

"How much have you learned so far?" Garrett asks.

"Not a thing. That's why I want to visit the vampires' club. Go straight to the source."

Garrett and Tank exchange glances. The big guy, second in the pack, nods at our alpha.

"All right." Garrett turns to Sheridan. "You'll go to the club."

"No." I swear to the fates, I'm ready to shift and fight right there. The thought of Sheridan toddling in there unprotected? I would burn the place down first.

"I can do it. I'll be all right," Sheridan says quickly.

Garrett points at me. "You'll go with her," he commands.

"No." It's Sheridan's turn to disagree.

"Yes," Garrett commands. I can't be sure, but I think a smile glimmers on Garrett's lips for a moment before disappearing. "I can't send you alone, Cuz. But Trey will be great back up. The vampires will know you're under both mine and Wolf Ridge's protection, and they'll think twice before messing with you."

"Fine." Sheridan nods.

"Fuck, no," I bite out.

Garrett turns to me. "Make sure no one lays a hand on her."

I groan again.

"And you"—Garrett rounds on Sheridan, and for the first time raises an eyebrow at her scandalous attire—"I know you're not my wolf, but this is my territory, and I'm responsible for you. Next time you plan on barging into a vampire meeting, you give me some fucking warning." His voice holds all the weight of his command.

"I will." Sheridan ducks her head. If she was in wolf form, she might put her tail between her legs. I'd be surprised, except Sheridan always cowed to authority, and Garrett has it in spades now that he's his own alpha.

"I know you can defend yourself pretty well, but do me a favor and stay close to Trey. I know you'll be tempted to give him a hard time—"

"Who, me?" She blinks innocently. I scowl.

"—But don't. It's dangerous enough going into the vampires' lair, backup or no backup," he lectures. "You both need to stick together and present a united front."

"Of course," Sheridan says, just as I mutter, "This is a mistake."

"You think I should send someone else?" Garrett asks. His tone is sharp, but I know he's really asking.

"No." I kick a rock with my boot with enough precision to send it rocketing into the air. "You're right."

There's no chance in hell I'd let her go with anyone else. I would go apeshit if I couldn't be beside her to protect her.

Besides, he and Tank are too high up in the pack to go to the club. Putting them in the vampires' clutches could invite assassination or kidnapping. We just declared peace, but it's best not to tempt the vampires too closely. An attack on a pack alpha or his second could mean war.

Jared might do it, if I asked, but he just took a mate. I'm single, expendable. And if I lose it and kick the shit outta a leech, the pack can write it off easier. Blame my bad temper, slap me on the wrist. As long as I beat up on a lesser leech, and don't go after Lucius himself.

"I'll do it," I tell my alpha.

Sheridan waits until Garrett looks away to flick a

brow at me. Wearing a sexy club get up instead of a stuck up suit really brings out the sass in her.

I gotta get her out of that outfit.

But not back into the suit.

Naked.

Fuck. No. Not that.

I'm staring at Sheridan. Her eyes widen as if she knows what I'm thinking, but she glares back with a shake of her head and makes another face.

Garrett catches her at it and frowns. "Behave."

"Of course." She smiles like a naughty angel. "Don't I always?"

Trey

"How'd you know we'd be here, anyway?" I ask Sheridan as I drop her off by her car in Fight Club's lot. After a few questions, Garrett and I discovered she didn't have her car, having walked. We took turns chewing her ear off before Garrett told me to give her a ride.

Which is how I ended up riding my bike back with Sheridan's arms around my waist and her soft body pressed into my back, fangs descending in my mouth and my dick ready to split the front of my jeans.

Lucky me.

"Sheridan?" I ask again, getting in her face so she can't dodge my question. "How did you know we were meeting the leeches in the wash?"

The way she hesitates before answering, I know I'm not going to like the answer.

"Nero," she admits. "It was the leech, Nero."

My curse echoes around the lot.

"Trey, I can handle it."

"Yeah? Why would he invite you to something like this?"

She nibbles her lip. "I don't know."

"Fuck, he's into you."

"You don't know that," she says quickly. "He probably just wanted to throw the Phoenix pack into the mix. Stir up trouble."

"Why would he do that?"

"I don't know." She glares at me like I'm the problem. "Why do leeches do anything?"

I curse some more, and kick gravel, wishing it was Nero's head. Or Lucius'. Don't care that touching the vampire king would start a war. If he messes with Sheridan, killing him would be worth it. "I don't like it."

Sheridan rolls her eyes. "I'm not crazy about him hanging around me either. Next time he touches me, I'll throw him into the bar." She rubs her wrist and my vision narrows, my wolf so close fur crackles along my forearm.

"Did he touch you? Fuck, Sheridan, these guys are dangerous—"

"You think I don't know that?" She gets back in my face, gesturing towards the building. "You're the one who lets them in. This place is crawling with them!"

"This area is no man's land. We're not on pack territory; otherwise Garrett would have to police us. This way we welcome everybody, but that means leeches and shifters are free to roam. I don't like it, but it's the way it's gotta be."

"And what do you get out of this?" She shifts closer, studying my face as if she really wants to know. "This place is a dump."

I step back, shutting down. "I guess that's where lowlifes like me belong." I don't think Sheridan really thinks that of me—at least she didn't when we were kids. But I'm parroting her dad, who never wanted me hanging around her.

"I didn't say that. I know you like to fight but…" She stops. "But this place, with the scary bouncer and leeches lurking in the corner, and the drunks. It's almost like you have a death wish."

"I'm not talking about it. It's none of your business. Besides, you can talk, accepting invites from vampires. What if he'd planned to get you alone and corner you?"

"I can take care of myself, Robson." Her lip curls. "You're not the only one who can fight."

I refrain from rolling my eyes, but only barely. Yes, she's a strong alpha female, but she's not invincible. There are dangers out there that go far beyond attending college out of state or running numbers for a brewery.

"Want me to prove it?"

I don't attempt to hide my exasperation. "No, Sheridan. I want you to stay out of fucking danger."

"You and me, in the ring," she challenges me.

Oh for fuck's sake. I hold up my hands. "Okay, sweetheart. You don't have to get defensive."

She crosses her arms over her chest. "This isn't defensive. This is me gearing up to kick your ass. Name the time and I'll come down here and get in the ring with you."

"Okay, okay, you can take care of yourself," I concede.

"Name the time, Robson." Her voice gets flinty. "I thought you loved sparring."

I stare at her for a long moment. I'd like to pretend I'm not imagining the two of us sliding around in a jello-pit, or mud-wrestling naked, but my dick thickens against my zipper. "Okay, fine. Tomorrow. Noon."

Her expression sears me like acid. "Get ready, Robson. Your ass is grass."

"I'm looking forward to it," I shoot back, and snarl at my own lame comeback.

"Tomorrow then."

"Fuck me," I mutter.

"No, thanks. Been there, done that, got the t-shirt." She tosses her hair and shrugs out of my jacket. "Here." Orange and vanilla wafts up from the leather, mingling with my scent. It smells good. Right. Meant to be.

We stare at each other over the piece of clothing, twelve years yawning between us. There's plenty of hurt and pain, but beneath the memories of how we hurt each other is more, so much more.

"Keep it," I tell her hoarsely. I like knowing she has something that belongs to me. Not much, but it's something.

She clutches the jacket to her chest and gives a curt nod. Something in me cracks a little, as if I'm relieved she didn't throw my gift back in my face. Fates, I'm still in deep with this woman.

I watch her strut to her car, hips twitching invitingly,

and clench my hands into fists. I don't know what I want to do more: strangle her or fuck her. Probably both. Yeah, that'd be good.

I hold my breath until the taillights of her car disappear. When I finally blow it out, I feel winded, like I've run for miles. Like I've been punched in the guts.

Sheridan Green. Fuck me. Fucking fuck me.

CHAPTER SIX

TWELVE YEARS AGO

I HEAD up the walk to my house, my lips curved with a secret smile. After school time used to be reserved for homework and studying the cramped pages of my text books until my vision blurred. Trey changed all that.

I take the steps two at a time, feeling loose and supple and full of light. My body sings the song of a well-satis-fied woman. I blush just thinking that. A woman, not a girl. Trey makes me feel alive.

My high lasts as long as it takes to turn the knob of the front door. As soon as I open it, my mom pops in front of me.

"Sheridan!" she cries. My dad looms behind her.

The smile falls from my lips. Fates, do they know where I've been?

"Mom? Dad?" I search their faces.

"So, when were you going to tell us?" my mom demands, and for a moment I'm about to pass out.

"About what?" I whisper, feeling sick. How did they find out about Trey? Did someone tell them?

A bright smile stretches my mom's mouth and I blink. There's no way she'd be smiling if she knew what I was doing after school with Trey.

"About *Stanford*, silly girl. Mrs. Stefani, the school counselor, called today to brag on you. Wolf Ridge is proud to graduate an Ivy league-bound senior!"

The nervous quiver I've had in my belly ever since Trey found the letter grows wilder, like a litter of eels circling around. "Well, I'm not sure about going."

My dad's smile flips to frown. "What are you talking about?"

"California's not that far away, honey," my mom says.

I fidget with the zipper on my backpack.

My dad's eyes narrow. "Is this about that Robson boy?"

My stomach sinks. "No," I lie.

Both my parents hear the untruth in my voice.

"Your future is way more important than a silly high school romance," my mom says.

"You're going," my dad insists. There's ice cold promise in his words, like he'll personally deliver me to school kicking and screaming if I refuse.

I try to appear unshaken, like this is still my decision, which it should be. I toss a casual shrug. "I sent in my acceptance but I'm still making up my mind." I attempt to infuse just enough brazenness in my words to sound like

I'm my own woman, and turn on my heel to head to my bedroom.

"Do not walk away when we're talking to you." And just like that, the conversation one-eighties from *we're proud of you* to *you're in deep shit, young lady.*

For the first time in my life, I consider running away. It's a rash and irrational thought, but it pops into my head immediately, like it's the only solution. I'm eighteen now —they shouldn't be running my life like this. Would Trey come with me if I did?

I stop and turn, teeth grinding. *"What?"* Yeah, I can play bitchy teen to a T.

"You're going to Stanford," my dad says. "There's nothing to decide."

I want to argue and fight, but my dad's pulling an alpha and I know there'd be no winning. Maybe that's why my brain produced running away as my only other option.

Tears of defeat pop into my eyes, but I don't let him see them, instead I whirl and run for my room, slamming the door like I'm thirteen again.

~

Present

I'M BACK at Fight Club at a quarter to noon. Daylight doesn't do this place any favors, but I can't help calculating the cost of pavement, new paint inside, maybe some bleachers around the cage...this place could be legit. Of course, I'd want to kick out the vampires, or maybe just make them sign something restricting their activity. Part of the thrill of this place is the danger; I wouldn't want to take that away completely.

My thoughts are swirling around waiver forms and liquor licenses and costs of regular powerwashing when my eyes land on Trey's tall form. He stands in a pool of light, dust motes dancing around his powerful body. His tattoos really aren't bad. Works of art, really. I want to peel off his clothes and make him tell me the stories of how, when and why he got them. Except that would mean he was naked.

No! Down girl. Bad idea.

"You ready for this?" he calls and I trot over to him. I'm wearing yoga pants and a loose top, my typical gym wear.

His forehead creases as he reads the words on my shirt. "You only do buttstuff at the gym?"

I grin. "I got this shirt from Etsy."

"Do you even know what *buttstuff* is?"

I stick my chin out, wishing my cheeks wouldn't color. "Yes. And I stand by my t-shirt's assertion. At least, for now." I bite the inside of my cheek after I add that last part. Trey's bemused expression changes to starved animal staring down its prey.

I clear my throat and pretend we weren't just dancing around the topic of anal sex. "Are we gonna do this in the ring? Fight, I mean?" I clarify, lest he's thinking I'm still talking about buttstuff.

Trey blinks and shakes himself like he's waking from a dream. Hopefully not a dream about bending me over, running his large hands up my legs and preparing me to take his cock in my...

Gah! Stop thinking about it.

"Uh, yeah. In the ring." He waves and I march inside the pen, glad for a chance to turn my back and hide my flaming face.

I've come to a realization in the last twelve hours since I saw him. Trey Robson is an itch, a big, annoying, delicious itch and sooner or later, I'm going to scratch. I know he's a player, I know it won't last. Twelve years ago he used up my love and threw me away.

But I'm a big girl now, and it's my turn to use him and walk away. I just gotta keep my pride and dignity intact. And, when it ends, my heart.

"Have you done this before?" he asks, coming into the caged area and closing the chain link door.

"Fought with you?"

"No." He frowns. "We fight all the time."

"Didn't used to though." I try to keep my voice breezy but fail.

"Whose fault is that?" He raises a blond brow. His eyes are ice cold.

I wrap my arms around myself to hide a shiver. "Fault goes both ways, I think."

"Yeah."

I'm surprised by his agreement, and we both look at the floor for a moment.

"How about this?" I walk to him and hold out my hand. "What's done is done. Truce?"

"Truce," he repeats softly and takes my hand. Just like that I'm falling, falling into the depths of his ocean eyes, falling for the magic of Trey. The touch of his fingers sings through me, pulling up all sorts of memories of when I wished he'd touch me forever. Twelve years after we walked away from each other, away from the ruin of our love, I wish he'd hung on tighter. Even after we hurt each other so completely, I could climb into his arms and never leave.

Trey drops my hand. The spell breaks. "Ready?"

"Yep." I bounce on the balls of my feet. If I can't hug him, I can hit him. I'd prefer that in the long run, anyway.

Then he pulls off his shirt.

"What..." My mouth is suddenly dry. "What are you doing?"

He drops his t-shirt at his feet, rubbing the tattoos on his arms absently. His lean muscles pop and flex, perfectly on display without him even trying. "Getting ready to fight, sweetheart."

I narrow my eyes. I want to call foul play, but then I'd have to admit the sight of him without his shirt affects me. "Should I take off mine then?"

His gaze darkens. "If you want."

I call his bluff, peel my shirt off and drop it on the floor next to his. My girls are stuffed into a hot pink sports bra, straining against the fabric, proudly on display.

It's Trey's turn to look dazed while I smirk at him. "Turnabout is fair play."

"Payback is a bitch," he retorts, but a smile dances around his mouth.

"Nope. Payback is a she-wolf named Sheridan." With fantastic tatas.

I turn from him and pretend to do some warm up stretches. I definitely don't bend and pause in positions that best showcase my butt. Of course not. That'd be cruel.

When I whirl back, he has his eyes closed and is pinching the bridge of his nose while taking deep breaths.

"Everything all right?" I ask with as much innocence as I can muster.

"Yeah. Just...yeah. All right." He drops his hand and looks everywhere but at my face, my hips, or my cleavage. "We'll start simple. I come at you, and you try to stop me."

"That's simple?" I ask dryly, but shrug. "Come on then."

"All right." He blows out a breath. Then he comes at me, eyes blazing. Muscles fill my vision and for a moment I panic—

Then my self-defense training kicks in. I step into him, grab his left hand, turn and pull him off balance, slamming my bottom into his hips and rolling him off my back. He slams into the ground. Before he recovers from the surprise, I drop a knee onto his chest, pinning him to the floor. "Yield!"

Trey stares up at me, making no move to try to fight me off or get the upper hand, even though I know he can. His nostrils flare, like he's breathing in my scent, and I see the flicker of silver in his eyes. His wolf is showing. After a beat, I lift off and back away.

"Where the fuck did you learn how to do that?"

"College," I shrug. "I took a few classes."

"Good thing you went, then." He winces right before I do.

I stare at him, something old and deep twisting in my gut. When he first broke up with me, I'd been sure it was

81

to make sure I went to Stanford. So I wouldn't give up the opportunity for him.

But then he—

Ugh. Water under the bridge. I don't want to think about it.

"Sorry. I just can't believe you—" He looks around the cage like he doesn't know how he got here. I would offer him a hand up, but I'm not sure it's a good idea to touch his skin. To get used to the feel of his hand in mine. The air between us crackles. "It's like you're a different person."

"Nope. Still me." I don't tell him that after we broke up, I examined my life. On the surface, I went to college and did everything to be the perfect she-wolf my parents raised me to be, but underneath, I was digging deep and discovering who I really was. I had Trey to thank, or blame, for the journey. He was the first wolf in my life who saw me, the real me, and loved me all the same. In the end, our relationship was a disaster, but also a gift. I had to give Trey up, but I found myself.

"I don't think I've ever seen you in a novelty t-shirt." He motions to the gym shirt crumpled on the floor. "Or that outfit last night. I would never guess you owned something like that."

"It's not my everyday office wear," I say, "But I like to have fun. You taught me that," I add, and flush. His particular brand of fun involved us on a motorcycle or somewhere with our clothes off.

"I don't think Garrett ever saw you wearing that much makeup. He almost didn't recognize you."

"I thought he looked surprised."

"Surprised? He almost shit his pants."

I chew the inside of my cheek.

"Oh that's right, you don't swear," Trey teases. "Someday I'm going to get you to say the 'f' word."

I roll my eyes.

"Come on," he wheedles. "Just once. Say it."

"All right, fine." I toss my head and announce, "The 'F' word."

Trey groans. "I'm going to make you say it. "

"Says the man who just got the wind knocked out of him on the floor."

"Someday. I'll catch you off guard. I'll make you scream it."

I narrow my eyes. "You will not."

"I will," he promises, his eyes hooded, gaze heavy on my face. My lips tingle. "Fuck, it'll be so hot."

Zing. Heat blooms between my legs at Trey's admission. I don't even know why he would think me saying the F word is hot, but knowing he does turns me on.

"Dream on, moonbrain," I reply primly, and we both burst out laughing. Trey stretches out on the mat and I lie down next to him, within arm's distance. It feels natural.

"Seriously, though," he says. "Why did you learn moves like that?"

"You really want to know? You have to promise not to freak out." At his sharp look, I sigh. "I had a stalker."

"What?" His whole body jerks and I throw out a hand.

"Relax. It's over. I took care of it."

His eyes are wolf bright. "Who was he?" he growls.

"Some dumb frat guy. Rich, privileged family. I think his mother was a judge. He was obviously used to getting his own way. He got me alone in a room one night. Upstairs from a party. The music was blaring, I guess so no one could hear me scream. He came at me, pushed me onto the bed." I pause, remembering that awful night.

"What happened?" Trey's voice is thick, his wolf close to the surface.

"I threw him through a window."

Trey blinks.

"*That which doesn't kill you, makes you stronger,*" I recite today's words of wisdom and shrug. "I'm not a victim, Trey. I'm a she-wolf. I have to act weak, protect the pack secret, but I was under attack. And he deserved it. The way he'd set up everything, he'd probably done it to other girls. I wanted to stop him."

"So you threw him from an upper story window?"

"It was only the second story," I defend. "He only broke both legs and an arm, a couple of ribs. We were able to write it off as an accident."

"You threw your stalker out a window," Trey says.

I hope I'm not imagining the glimmer of pride in his tone. "Yep." I raise my chin and own it. "I defenestrated him. *Defenestrate* means *To throw out a window,*" I explain while Trey looks blank. "I learned that from a Word a Day calendar."

"You and your calendars." Trey shakes his head, but the corner of his mouth quirks up.

"Now are you ready to believe me when I say I can handle some vampires?"

He hangs his head. "I guess. I don't like it, but...damn."

"What?"

"You've changed. I like it. I like it. A lot."

"Thanks." I want to turn away, hide how much his opinion means to me. Before I can, he raises a large hand halfway to my face, and stops. I freeze, staring down at him. After a moment, he pushes a lock of hair off my cheek and tucks it behind my ear.

"Sheridan," he murmurs. "Sheridan Green. Where have you been hiding?"

Right where you left me, I want to scream. *Back in Wolf Ridge, picking up the pieces of my broken heart.*

Instead of shouting, I shudder as his thumb rubs my lower lip. His touch goes right through me, tingling lower down.

"You always were so sweet. But also wild," his voice deepens. "At least, you were with me."

This is Trey! The sane part of me screams. *He's a player! He wrote the player playbook!*

The rest of me sighs as he cups the back of my neck, drawing me closer. His eyes are the blue of faraway tropical waters and my brain wants to take a vacation.

"So naughty. And nice. And..." His lips brush my mouth and I close my eyes. "Open, open," he whispers, and I obey, my lips seeking his, my mind dizzy and grasping his commands like a lifeline. "Yes, that's it, sweetheart. Just like that." He deepens the kiss, his big hand threading through my hair and angling my head where he wants it. I relax and let him take control, my whole body singing, sighing, drinking every word and touch and whisper until I'm floating.

"Trey," I breathe and he answers me with another small kiss. This is crazy. We're supposed to be fighting. We were fighting and then what happened? Trey magic.

He draws back and I moan a little, following him with my mouth. I'm supposed to be strong. What was I doing? I can be strong.

I break the kiss. He doesn't force anything more, just tips my head forward until my forehead touches his, and shakes his head slowly. We stay like that moment, breath mingling, moving in sync.

The thick scent of my own lust hits me, and I draw back. Trey releases me, and I scramble into a sitting position, breathing hard even though we haven't been moving. I wish I had some words of wisdom right now, but all I can think of is a variation on *Give a man a fish...*

Give a player a kiss, and he owns you. Teach a player to kiss, and he locks lips with every freakin' female in a hundred mile radius...

I clear my throat, searching for my voice. "So are you convinced?"

"What?" he blinks.

"That I can take care of myself. Cause if you are, I, um, got to go."

He props himself up on an elbow, beautiful face still composed.

I grab my shirt and practically run from the cage, only stopping when I'm home free.

"I'll see you Saturday. At the vamp club. Eight p.m. If you're not there, I'll wait ten minutes, and go in without you."

"The fuck you will," he growls as I leave the building. But he's not the boss of me.

I just have to remember that.

CHAPTER SEVEN

TWELVE YEARS AGO

I PULL my beat up motorcycle around to the side exit of Wolf Ridge High and lean on one foot, waiting. Sheridan comes out alone and heads straight for me, not like she's happy to see me, more like she's eager to put distance between her and school.

Her expression is closed and she doesn't smile or kiss me before she swings a muscular thigh over the back of my bike and climbs on.

Something's eating her.

I'm a quiet guy myself, so I don't waste words on asking about it now. She'll tell me when she's ready.

I hand her a helmet and wait until it's on before I take off. I decide to skip our usual haunts—Vitale's pizza or Wolf Ridge Cafe—and drive straight for the mountains.

I know when I'm out of sorts, letting my wolf out heals me. Once we take the turnoff for the mountains, I gun it, letting the sensation of wind across our faces simulate a four legged run. I think that's why young wolves love motorcycles so much. We're physical creatures. We sense everything in our bodies, and keeping them cooped up in buildings or cars makes us tense.

I spin all the way to the top of the first foothill and park. Sheridan climbs off and tosses her backpack on the table, then climbs up and sits on it, her feet resting on the bench. She stares out over the rocky desert terrain.

I sit beside her and gently bump shoulders.

"Hey."

"My brother died today."

Oh.

I understand what she means. Today marks the anniversary of his death, not the actual day he died. Her brother, Zach, had been a rising star in the pack. Four years older than us, he'd been the football quarterback and valedictorian, had a full ride to Pepperdine. He died in a motorcycle accident the summer after his senior year. Even a shifter can't survive getting his skull crushed.

"You miss him?"

Her face crumples and she draws in a hiccupy breath. "A lot. We were close, actually."

I weave my fingers through hers and just sit with her, listening to the birds call, the distant swish of traffic below.

"Do you ever worry about my motorcycle?" I've thought of this before, but hadn't wanted to bring it up.

She never acted afraid, so I figured it wasn't an issue. But since we're talking about Zach, it's worth discussing.

"No. I actually love that you ride a bike. It reminds me of him in a good way. He used to give me rides all the time when he was still learning. He even taught me to drive it myself, against our parents' wishes."

I squeeze her hand.

"I don't worry about you, because you're careful. You don't drink and drive. You wear a helmet. You take it seriously."

"He didn't?"

She shakes her head. "He thought he was invincible. No helmet, crazy driving after drinking—you get the picture." She stands up and swivels, surprising me by straddling my waist.

I palm her ass and yank her closer before I even think about whether it's inappropriate considering what she's going through. She seems to be on board, though. She twines her arms around my neck and kisses me.

My hormones kick in immediately and my cock stiffens in the notch between her legs. I slide a hand up her t-shirt to palm her breast.

She rocks against me. We've been playing this way for a while—second base mostly. Dry humping, some groping. I got close to third once—I am dying to give her pleasure with my mouth—but she got skittish and pushed me away. I totally respect that.

"I'm ready, Trey," she whispers in my ear.

My head snaps up, dick lurches painfully against my jeans.

"I bought condoms."

If this was a cartoon, I'd be comically spluttering like a stunned idiot. Never in a million years did I dream she'd spring this on me. Especially on a day like this.

I vowed never to try anything when she'd been drinking, but my girl is dead sober. And sad. And she wants me to make it better.

I sure as hell can do that.

"Are you sure?" It comes out as a hoarse croak.

She leans forward and bites my neck. "Yeah. I want to *live*. I can't just turn off all fun to get to the future Zach didn't have." She closes her eyes and shakes her head. "Does that make sense?"

"Yeah." I'm breathing hard, my body already springing into animal mode. I spin her around and hold my hand behind her head as I push her to her back on the table. I'm over her in a second.

It's my first time, but my body knows what to do. Or maybe it's my wolf. I kiss down her neck. Nip her breast.

She moans and arches up from the table.

I shove her t-shirt up to her armpits and free her breasts from her hot pink bra. They're fucking perfect. Just enough to fill my hands, youthful and firm. Her stiff nipples grow even harder when I suck on them.

"The condoms are in my bag," Sheridan whispers. "Outer pocket."

Damn. She came prepared. Or did she plan it? How long have those condoms been in there? I don't tell her I bought a box a few months ago, too, just in case this moment ever came.

"I'll get them in a minute," I murmur, and trail my tongue down her flat belly, swirling it in the indent of her belly button. The scent of her arousal tickles my nose and my body reacts like it was a kick of amphetamine.

Present

Trey

I DREAM about Sheridan all night, but they're not the wet dreams of my youth. They're fucking angsty and painful. She's flipping me on my back and kicking my ribs over and over again, sobbing. She's getting captured and hauled off by the nest of vampires, and there's nothing I can do to keep her safe. Her dad catches me in bed with her and tortures my mom to punish me.

I wake with my psyche bruised and battered. The need to take care of Sheridan—to fix things once and for all consumes me. But what good will it do? Yeah, I purposely drove us apart because I wanted the best for her. It might help her to know that. To know I never stopped loving her.

Hell, I've never even been with another girl since her. My wolf wouldn't accept it. He wanted Sheridan from the first day he saw her and he wouldn't let me sully the memory of her with anyone else. The pack calls me 'the monk.'

But why stir up the past? Nothing's changed. Sheridan's still the pack princess. Her father's still never going to accept me as her mate. Making sure she went to Stanford didn't win me any points with her or him. It just solidified our differences.

I climb out of bed and step into the shower. Sheridan's fucking everywhere in my head—she surrounds me, my thoughts swirling in an endless loop of worry around her.

And then it hits me why.

It's October 25th. The anniversary of her brother's death. My mate is suffering.

I slam off the water and grab a towel. I don't give a shit what went down between us. I don't care if a future's impossible. If Sheridan needs me, it would take every pack on Earth to keep me away.

I pull on a pair of jeans and a t-shirt and one of my leather jackets and go outside. Thank fuck I asked Sheridan where she was staying. I get on my bike and drive to Meyer Street, going up and down until I see her car parked in front of one of the casitas.

I verify it's her place by the sweet vanilla-orange scent and walk up to the door.

It's only then it occurs to me that she might not appreciate my support. But fuck it—I have to offer.

I knock. She comes to the door, heart-breakingly lovely. Her caramel-hued hair falls around her shoulders and she's wearing a soft, mauve t-shirt that molds to her ample breasts, and a pair of skinny jeans that look like pure sin on her. But she's not her usually, snappy, together self. There's a subdued quality to her that makes my heart twist.

I was right to come.

"Trey?" Her honey and peaches voice is soft and puzzled.

I flip the motorcycle keys around my finger. "Want to go for a ride?"

Her eyes fly open in surprise, confusion and wonder warring in her expression. She tilts her head to the side. "Why?"

I shrug. "I know this day is hard for you."

Her beautiful face instantly crumples. Tears pop in her eyes and she falls into my arms. "I can't believe you remembered."

I stroke her silky hair. "Yeah, of course I remembered, baby." I breathe in her scent. "Of course I did."

Her back shakes on a silent sob. "I still miss him," she chokes, her tears wetting my neck.

I slip my hand under her hair and massage her neck. "I know," I murmur.

After a moment, she gets it back together, sniffs and pulls away, ducking her head. "I'll go get my shoes on."

I'm almost lightheaded with relief—she's coming with me. She's letting me offer this comfort to her today.

I'm not foolish enough to believe this means anything in the grand scheme of things, just grateful I get to be with her today.

She comes back, wearing my jacket and her sexy club boots. She's put lip gloss on, which makes my damn dick forget that she was just crying two seconds ago.

I hold my hand out and she curls her fingers into mine, letting me lead her out of the casita to my bike parked on the street behind her car. "Where to? Mountains?"

"Have you eaten?"

I shake my head. "Nope. Wanna get food first?"

93

She takes the helmet I offer her and tosses her hair back before putting it on. "Definitely."

I take her to a nouveau Mexican restaurant on Broadway where we both get heaping plates of huevos rancheros smothered in salsa verde and extra avocado. She shovels the food in her mouth like the healthy shifter she is.

"I didn't think I could eat today, but suddenly I'm starving," she says between bites.

I smile. *Adorable wolf.* "Good. Eat up."

She wipes her lips on her napkin. "So, how much do you bring in a week with Fight Club?"

Oh boy. Here comes MBA Sheridan, with that brilliant mind and laser focus pinpointed right on me.

I shrug. "Enough."

She takes a large gulp of ice water. "No really. Let's talk numbers. I'll bet there's places to improve profitability."

I raise a brow. "Thought you were gonna try to shut me down."

Something flickers over her face—regret, maybe. She drops her eyes to her food and scoops another forkful. "That may not be necessary."

"Mm," I grunt in response.

"You're not going to tell me?"

"What?"

"Your numbers? Let's see, I would say Luka and I rang up about $900 in drinks Wednesday night and the margin's probably around thirty percent. So $600 profit. You had five people on staff, including me. What does that eat up?"

I'm incapable of denying her this chew-toy for her brain. "Two hundred. Fifty bucks to each of the security guys, twenty-five base pay for the bartenders. I'll get your breakfast," I say wryly, since she never got paid.

She rolls her eyes. "I don't care about that. I made a ton in tips, anyway."

"So four hundred after paying staff. Do you pay the fighters?"

I shake my head. "That's a separate business enterprise."

"Financed through illegal betting?"

Of course she's too damn smart to miss what's going on. I give a ghost of a shrug as acknowledgement.

"So four hundred a night. What's the overhead on the building?"

"We own it, so it's just three hundred a month in utilities."

Her brows shoot up. I shouldn't be pleased to see she's impressed, but they are half-million dollar warehouses. I'm not the poor, scrappy kid whose mom works the lowest job in the pack anymore.

"You own it personally?"

"Jared and I own both warehouses on the lot. His mate uses the other one as a dance studio and performance space."

"Really? Wow. I'd like to see it."

"I'm sure Angelina would be happy to show you around." For a brief moment, I ride the high of picturing Angelina and Sheridan hitting it off and the four of us becoming happy couple friends.

That's not happening. Sheridan's going back to Wolf Ridge, where she'll eventually be running the entire show.

I'll be here running Fight Club.

"Anyway, with you owning the building, the opportunity for profit is huge. You just need to maximize the number of shifters who come through that door, and give them good reason to stay—whether it's the fights or other entertainment. And of course, keep the trouble out." She frowns and my gut tightens.

I throw down some cash on the table. "Ready for a ride?"

She nods. "So ready. Where are we going?"

"Gates Pass." At her questioning look, I grin. "You'll love it, come on."

SHERIDAN

RIDING on the back of Trey's motorcycle for the second day in a row has my heart somersaulting. I was too melancholy to get horn-gry riding with him to the restaurant, but now the giant vibrator between my legs and the familiar scent of Trey and his leather have me rocking my hips over the bike seat. My breasts press up against his back, arms loop around his washboard abs.

I still can't believe he remembered.

I mean, I know today marks the anniversary of the day he took my V-card, but I doubt he marked it on a calendar to celebrate every year. Especially considering how easily he was finished with me at the end of senior year.

My brain wants to tear at this puzzle until I have it solved or demolished, but I keep pushing it away. If I think too much about Trey and his actions toward me, I'll end up twelve years in the past with my heart beaten to a bloody pulp.

No, better to just be in the now. Appreciate Trey showing up for me when I needed him. Allow the suffocating heaviness of the day to lift and move off me.

He drives west, toward the Tucson mountain range and takes me up a beautiful mountain pass. The air smells fresh and clean. Saguaro cacti shimmer and glow in the warm autumn sun. Trey drives through the pass and down the other side, then parks at the trailhead for King Canyon. It's Friday—a work day for most of Tucson—so the lot is empty except for Trey's bike.

My wolf starts wagging her tail in anticipation of being out in nature.

Trey takes my hand and we walk up the trail, cutting through the desert. He doesn't speak, and for once, I keep my mouth shut, too. Suddenly, there's nothing to be or prove with Trey. Our silence is companionable. Honoring.

We reach a saddle, an incredible overlook over the city of Tucson. Trey starts kicking off his boots as he pulls his shirt over his head.

For one stupid second, I think he wants to have sex— like he expects it because that's what we did on the last anniversary of my brother's death. But he grins at me. "Last one on four legs is a rotten egg."

"No fair," I holler, because he already has a head start. I scramble out of my clothes and shift, then bound over his wolf as I tear up Wassan Peak.

We run for hours, nipping and playing, sniffing. Hunting.

And then it all ends when I get my nose into a cholla cactus. It's idiotic. The first lesson I learned as a cub growing up in Arizona was to stay away from cholla—also known as jumping cactus because of the way the giant burrs jump from the mother and attach their barbs into passersby.

I yelp at the pain—mostly because it's my tender nose and the face is so personal. Pain there is so intense. In the blink of an eye, Trey shifts and crouches beside me, concern etched in his face.

I whimper, trying to paw the damn thing off, which only gets more burrs stuck in my paws.

"Easy, baby. Let me." Trey—the idiot—grabs the thing with his *fingers* and pries it off my nose. I yelp again, but it's only partly out of pain, partly out of concern for him, because now *he* has the burr firmly embedded in his hand, which means he won't be able to shift and run back to where we left our clothes.

He's totally unfazed, though. He just strokes my ear with his good hand. "Are you okay?" He leans close to examine my snout and paws. "Any left?" I lick his face and he laughs and rubs my cheek.

I sit and wait as he pries the cactus ball from his hand with a stick, then uses his teeth to pull out the remaining barbs.

"All better." He holds up his bloodied palm for me to see and I lick it, too.

In a flash, he's back on all fours, running down the mountain.

I give an indignant, joyful bark and bound after him, down the mountain, passing his sleek white and silver form just before we reach the saddle.

I shift back, laughing, and yank on my clothes. "Beat you."

He shifts and pulls on his jeans, too. "Of course you did." The satisfaction in his tone tells me he let me win, just like he let me throw him yesterday at the gym.

Just like he let you think he was interested in playing the field, my wolf whispers.

But no. That's dangerous, wishful thinking. I spent hundreds of hours in college sitting in my dorm trying to talk myself into believing that. But it didn't matter. Because even if it were true, I made sure he'd never speak to me again.

But he's here now, she whispers.

Yes. He's here now. Does that mean he's forgiven me?

Have I forgiven him?

Stop thinking. Stop thinking. Just enjoy this moment.

We hike back to the bike in the same comfortable silence. Ride back to my place. Trey doesn't get off his bike, like he's just dropping me off. Definitely not expecting sex.

The disappointment spearing my mid-section tells me I was hoping for it.

"You want to come in?" Oh crap. Do I sound desperate? He should be begging me, not the other way around.

His eyes flash silver. "Fuck, Sheridan. Of course I do."

"But?"

He shakes his head. "I can't." He sounds pained.

"Why not?"

His breath has grown quicker, the veins in his neck are popping out. "I have to get to Fight Club. We have an event."

"Want me to work?"

"No." His answer is quick and definitive, which hurts way more than I want to admit. "Nope, we're all set," he says, like he's trying to soften it.

"But I'll see you tomorrow for the leech thing."

Something tight coils in my gut. "Right. Sure." I turn and walk up the path to my casita without saying goodbye.

Trey's up to something. He doesn't want me at the club tonight. Why? Is it a woman? Or something with the vampires?

Whatever it is, I'm going to find out.

I'll be darned if he can keep me out.

Trey

OH HOLY HELL.

Was Sheridan actually inviting me into her place...for *sex*?

Damn, the girl never stops surprising me.

It took every grain of willpower in me not to pick her

up, carry her inside and mark her as forever mine. Because that's what will happen if we ever get naked again together.

But she's weak today. She's grieving. I may not have been strong enough to resist her offer as a teenager, but I'm sure as hell not going to take advantage now.

Especially when I have no chance of keeping her as mine.

Because I'm definitely not okay with a little recreational sex. There's no such thing for my wolf. He wants me to claim Sheridan. Mark her. Make her mine forever.

Which means I need to keep a very healthy distance between us. Before I fuck everything up between us.

Again.

CHAPTER EIGHT

TWELVE YEARS AGO

 *heridan*

TREY GROWLS when I pop the button of my jeans, then shimmy them down my hips. Young she-wolves are warned against fooling around with pubescent boys—they can easily lose control, but Trey's not a boy.

He's all beautiful man and other than the growl, he's showing major restraint, considering I just gave him the green light.

He kisses my pussy over my panties, gently bites my inner thigh. He rubs his thumb over the satin, finding the place that makes me squirm. It's unbelievably intense. I've never been touched there by another person and the urge to shove him away before I lose myself is almost as great as the searing pleasure his touch brings.

"Trey," I moan.

"Fuck yeah, baby. You can say my name like that any time." He slips his thumb under my panties and strokes over my slit.

My belly shudders in on a breath and I squirm. Trey wraps an arm around one of my thighs and dives between my legs. I'm totally unprepared for the shock of his tongue on my most sensitive bits.

I squeal and jerk, but he holds me still, tortures me with quick flicks to what must be my clit—I should probably know where it is, but I don't—then flattens his tongue and licks into me. He traces my inner lips, penetrates my opening.

I moan and sigh and writhe beneath him. "Trey, the condoms."

He lifts his head and chuckles. "You in a hurry to get to the finish line, baby?"

My laugh is a release of nervous tension. "Maybe. I have a lot of anticipation rolled into this."

He screws one finger into me and I jack off the table with a cry. The fit is tight and a little intense, but it also feels so right. He slides it in and out slowly, and I let my head tilt back. My eyes roll upward under my closed lids.

I knew sex would feel good. I just didn't know it would feel this good. And we haven't even gotten to the main course yet.

Trey adds a second finger and I whimper, not because it hurts, but because the intensity doubles. When he pumps now, I start to moan on each exhale.

Trey drags my backpack over with his free hand and I grab it and fish out the box of condoms, then hand him one. He's still in no hurry, though. He ducks his head and sucks one nipple while he moves his fingers in and out of me.

I snatch the condom out of his hand and rip it open. "Please, Trey," I moan.

He growls and takes the rubber, then shoves his jeans down enough to free his erection. For a lean, muscled guy, his cock seems out of proportion big. Not that I have anything to compare it to.

He rolls on the condom and climbs over me. I spread my knees wide and reach for him. He claims my mouth with passion, kissing and sucking my lip and—oh fates! He spears me with his erection, entering me with one swift stab.

I cry out from the flash of pain, but once he's in, he doesn't move, except to stroke my hair back from my face and gaze into my eyes. "You okay, baby?"

My entire body trembles, heat cascades through me. I give a shaky nod. He smiles and rocks his hips, easing out just a bit before pushing back in.

Yes.

This time it feels right. Satisfying. So good.

"Again," I urge.

He repeats the action and my toes curl. I moan. He continues, gently rocking, filling me, stroking my insides with his thick length.

I'm nearly out of my mind, but somehow he's still able to lower his head and worry one nipple with his tongue, his teeth.

I dig my nails into his shoulders, hook my feet around his back to pull him in tighter, demanding, "Faster."

He curses and braces his torso above me, thrusting with more force.

It's shockingly too much and so delicious. The head of his cock hits something inside me—my cervix?—but I ignore the dull ache it causes, and keep pulling Trey into me.

"Sheridan," he rasps. His voice is gravelly and pained. His eyes shine silver, his wolf surging to the surface. I wonder if mine have changed, too.

The muscles in Trey's back and shoulders flex into hard rocks. The world spins around me. I close my eyes, throw my head back with pleasure.

Trey shouts, pounding harder into me and then thrusting deep and staying. His muscular ass squeezes as he comes. Without fully understanding what's happening, my body knows the exact response. An orgasm explodes, my internal muscles clenching around his cock, milking more of his cum from him.

For a few moments, I'm nowhere. Just floating, spinning, enjoying the reverberations of pleasure as my breath gradually slows, my heart stops thundering.

Trey strokes the hair back from my face, caresses my cheek. I blink my eyes open and I'm shocked to find his irises still gleaming silver, his canines spiked as if he wanted to mark me. I realize his body is shaking above me, muscles corded up as if the effort of holding back from marking me is killing him.

And yet he continues to show me only gentleness. He has the control not to take the step that would bind us together for the rest of our lives.

Make me his forever.

My heart beats fast at the knowledge that his wolf picked me for its mate. Does my wolf concur? How would I know? Female wolves don't mark their mates. There isn't a special serum to embed in our mates' skin.

Regardless of what my wolf thinks, I know without a shadow of a doubt, that the idea of Trey marking me is nothing but exciting. In fact, I'm soaring, as if he'd just declared his undying love. Pledged his life and soul to me.

I touch his clenched jaw. "I think your wolf likes me." I say it lightly, acknowledging it to prevent any awkwardness.

He pulls out and rolls off me, standing up to remove the condom and zip his pants. "So fucking much." He slides my panties up, then my jeans, then pulls me to sitting. He stands between my thighs and holds me, his palms stroking my back, my hair. He kisses my head. "Thank you, Sheridan."

My heart stutters in my chest. Every kid or adult in Wolf Ridge who thinks Trey is just some hardened asshole because of his fights, or who his dad was or his lack of achievement ought to know this side of him. Tender, grateful. Sweet.

I lift my lips for him to kiss, and think if we were cat shifters, I'd definitely be purring right now.

Present

SHERIDAN

I SHOW up at Fight Club in a short red corduroy mini skirt and a silky black blouse that leaves one shoulder bare.

Jared's at the front door and he moves to bodily block my entrance. "Oh no. No way I'm letting you in there tonight."

Just as I thought—something's going on.

"Why not?" I try to skirt around him, but he shifts to block me again. I put my hands on my hips.

"Nope. Trey does not need you distracting him. Sorry, Sheridan. Come back another night."

I lift my chin. "I'm going in there. Trey's a big boy, he doesn't need you to protect him from me."

Jared fights a smile. "Yeah, I think he does. And I have money riding on Trey tonight, so I'm really protecting my own interests here."

I go still. "Trey's fighting?"

Jared closes his eyes, turns and smacks his head against the door frame. "I'm sure you weren't supposed to know that. Now turn around and drive back home, Sheridan."

"Why wouldn't he want me to know?" My heart's beating faster, but I'm not sure why.

Jared rubs his jaw. "You'd have to ask Trey that—but not tonight," he adds quickly. "You can ask him tomorrow. After he wins this fight."

Grizz comes out and glances at both of us. "Five minutes," he mutters to Jared.

Five minutes until fight time? I need in there. The thought of Trey in the cage both terrifies and turns me on. And there's no way I'm not going to see it.

I make another attempt to slip by Jared while he's distracted with Grizz, but he's way too fast.

"Jared!" I growl.

He shrugs with a smug smile. "No one to run and tattle to down here, is there? Maybe you should go back home."

I ignore the jab. Yes, I clearly need to make amends with the Tucson pack, but that's not going to happen tonight. Tonight, I'm getting into Fight Club to see Trey in the ring.

"What makes you think Trey wouldn't win if I'm in there?" I demand. I can't decide whether to be pissed off or flattered.

Jared leans a hand against the doorframe and blows out an exasperated breath. "Sheridan, if you're in there, Trey's gonna be worried about your safety—who's talking to you, who's touching you, whose throat he needs to rip out. He's not gonna be focused on his opponent and winning the fight."

"I won't let him see me," I wheedle. "I'll stay in a back corner until after the fight. Just *let me in*, Jared."

The crunch of a heavy boot sounds behind me and I turn to see my cousin Garrett coming up the walk. "What's going on?"

I swallow. This is going from bad to worse.

Jared tips his head at me. "She wants in. I said no."

I grind my teeth.

Garrett's lips twitch. "Sucks when you're not the one in charge for a change, doesn't it?"

My brain lights on an idea. I hook my hand around Garrett's huge arm. "I'll stick with Garrett," I promise. "I won't let Trey see me, but if he does, he'll know I'm totally safe with your alpha."

Jared glances at Garrett, who shrugs. "Fine," he grumbles. "But if Trey loses this fight because you're here, I will be collecting my losses from *you*."

"Fine." I hurry in behind Garrett, sticking close to his side, as promised.

Trey's already in the cage, Grizz announcing the contestants.

Garrett elbows his way to a high-top table in the back corner. "I'd ask if you want a drink, but then I'd have to leave you unattended, and it sounds like I'm your babysitter tonight."

I roll my eyes. "Go get a drink. I can take care of myself."

The crowd shouts as Grizz blows a whistle and the first punches are thrown, and I forget the tension between me and my cousin, or Jared, or the rest of the pack. All my attention is on the beautiful fighter pivoting and punching in the cage. Trey's a big guy, but not thick, like Jared, or Garrett or Grizz. He's lean and sinewy. Pure grace. Pure focused energy. He moves quickly, his long arms delivering punches that flatten his opponent, a short, stocky cat shifter, if I'm not mistaken.

Cage fighting is wild and rough. When the cat shifter leaps up, he appears close to shifting—eyes glinting green and his hair standing up on his nape. He throws himself at Trey, tackling him with a wrestling move.

Trey flips him over, cuts off his air flow with an arm against his throat, waits until the guy smacks the floor to let him up.

I hold my breath, but I'm not afraid.

I'm in awe.

They both get up and Trey bounces on his feet, his eyes lit with total focus. It's his lips that catch my attention, though. They're curling up at the edges.

Trey's enjoying himself.

Of course he is.

How could I have forgotten what fighting means to him? It's how he lets off steam.

I smile, too, my body tingling with awareness of his male virility, his unbridled power.

The fight's over too soon. I could've watched Trey fight all night, but his opponent went down and wouldn't get up.

Grizz takes Trey's bare fist—no boxing gloves for this rowdy bunch—and holds it in the air.

The crowd cheers and I clap, jumping to see over their heads. Garrett grabs my waist and lifts me high in the air. As my head pops over the crowd, Trey sees me. Our eyes lock, and I watch his face split into a grin right before Garrett drops me to the ground again.

I take off, pushing through the crowd. Garrett curses, staying at my back until the crowd parts for Trey—shirtless, bloodied, magnificent.

Trey

NEVER IN A MILLION years would I have guessed Sheridan

would enjoy watching me fight. She must, though, because she launches herself right at me. I pick her up, wrap those muscular legs around my back and carry her to my office like a conquering Viking.

She laughs in my ear, low and husky. Her scent's up in my nostrils—vanilla, orange and the feminine musk of her arousal.

Shit.

"Why didn't you tell me?" she breathes against my neck as I kick the door shut.

I push her back against the wall and grind into the notch of her legs. "Tell you what?"

"You were fighting. Why didn't you want me to know?"

I slide my hands up under her shirt, groan when I find she's braless. I squeeze her ample breasts, rub my thumbs over her nipples. "I didn't know you'd like it." My voice sounds rough to my own ears. I scrape my teeth along her neck, suck her earlobe into my mouth.

Her hips jerk and she grinds over my throbbing dick.

"Thought you'd hate it, actually."

"Why?"

I thrust mindlessly into the notch of her legs like I'm going to dry fuck her right to orgasm. Her shirt ends up at her armpits, exposing the most beautiful pair of tits. They're a little bigger than they were in high school, and fuck if that doesn't send another rocket of lust barreling through me.

I ease her feet to the floor so I can get my fingers between her legs. *Oh sweet honey*—she's so wet for me. I shove her panties to the side and stroke her plump folds.

"Condom?" Sheridan pants.

Condom. Fuck!

I growl and screw one finger into her tight channel. So I'll just have to get her off. "I don't have one," I admit.

She whimpers.

"It's okay, baby." I pump my index finger in and out of her, then curl it toward her front wall, trying to find her G-spot. "I can still take care of your needs."

She clutches my shoulders, digs her nails into my bare skin.

A growl rockets from my throat, my vision domes. Somehow I manage to drag in a breath and focus. I slide a second finger in her and mold my hand over her mons, grinding my palm down on her clit. Her muscles clench as I thrust my fingers in and out. I try for the G-spot again, and this time I find it, the place where the tissue stiffens up.

I swallow her cry with my mouth, kissing her like my life depends on it. Like the taste of her will heal me. Give me new life.

Maybe it will.

Maybe it will be the death of me. Hard to say. All I know is right now, watching Sheridan come is the only drug I crave. I twist my lips over hers, claiming her mouth with a bruising intensity, all the while working my fingers, the heel of my hand. When I find her nipple and pinch—hard—she throws her head back and screams.

I continue stroking my fingers in and out of her, pressing on her clit until her muscles stop squeezing, She falls forward against me, panting.

"Trey."

I thread my fingers up the back of her hair and breathe in Sheridan. My fingers are still curled inside her like they belong there permanently. I slowly ease out and bring them to my mouth, sucking her essence off my fingers one by one, all the while holding her gaze.

"You don't have a condom?" Her voice is scratchy from screaming and there's a dazed quality to her gaze that makes my wolf preen.

I did that to her.

But apparently it wasn't enough. "No, baby. Want me to go beg one off Jared?"

She flushes and shakes her head. "Fates, no." She shoots a thoughtful gaze at me—seeing far too much. "Why don't you have one, Trey?"

I go still. I want to tell her, but my wounds are still too raw. My intentions for her, too deep.

"Aren't you the big player?"

I stumble back like she punched me. Regret instantly seeps over her expression.

I just shake my head.

She steps forward. "No?"

"Let's not do this, Sheridan."

Pain flits over her face. "Right. Let's not." She pulls her blouse back down over her breasts, straightens her skirt.

"Well… thanks. It was nice to see you fight. And, um, this"—she flushes and makes a flitting gesture to the room — "was, ah..."

I press my lips back over hers. "Don't."

She looks up at me, eyes wide, expectant. Like I'm supposed to lead wherever the hell we're going.

And I have no fucking clue.

I kiss her again. It's not the same claiming kiss of before. More of a firm seal. Like putting a finish on something. We did this.

Now it's over.

We probably shouldn't do it again.

"Thanks for coming to see me." *I love you.* "I'll walk you out to your car." *I'm letting you go.*

CHAPTER NINE

TWELVE YEARS AGO

SHERIDAN'S HOUSE isn't a mansion, but to a kid who grew up in a double wide on the wrong side of the tracks, it might as well be. My scuffed boots tread the gleaming tile lightly even though there's no one around but us. Her dad's at work and her mom took her sister to Tucson for some all-day gymnastics tournament. I sort of hate being here, because I know her dad would kick my ass if he found me , but I think that's part of the thrill for Sheridan. She likes the naughtiness of fucking under her parents' roof, and I'm not gonna deny her a single fantasy.

I walk around her bedroom, examining the childhood treasures and young adult books. I see a paper tucked under her desk calendar, like it's something secret, and I slide it out.

"Oh!" Sheridan catches sight of it at the same time I realize what it is.

An acceptance letter for college. From Stanford.

"Holy shit, Sheridan—why didn't you tell me about this?"

We never talk about next year—about what's going to happen when she goes to college and I stay here, peddling pot and working on motorcycles with Garrett and Jared. I've tried to bring it up a couple times, but she always clams up and changes the subject.

"Why haven't you accepted this yet?" I see the blank form underneath the letter, the one she's supposed to send back to confirm her place.

She snatches the paper away from me. "I'm not going." Her brows are down. "I have a scholarship to ASU."

"Yeah, but this is an Ivy league school, baby. You should be jumping on this."

She narrows her eyes. "Why would I want to leave Arizona?"

My breath whooshes out of me, because—yeah—I don't want her to leave the state, either. But I also don't want her giving up her life for me. Or maybe it's not for me. I guess I need to find out.

"Why wouldn't you?" I challenge.

She's breathing fast, her breastbone rising and falling, tempting my eyes toward her cleavage, but I don't give in. "You."

Fuck. She said it. I can't stop the explosion of warmth in my chest, nor can I help the goofy grin that spreads across my face.

"Give me that." I snatch the letter out of her hand and

slap it down on the desk. Then I tug her arm to position her in front of it. She's not expecting what happens next. Maybe I'm crazy to do it, but I push her torso down and smack her ass.

There's a shocked gasp—maybe from both of us—and I don't move. I guess I'm waiting to see if she turns around and punches me in the face. When she stays still, I smack her again, and again.

"That's for not telling me you got into fucking Stanford," I lecture her as I spank her, picking up the intensity as I gain confidence.

"And that's for trying to deflect an incredible opportunity." I kick her feet apart and slap between her legs. My cock is rock hard now and I'm fucking loving dishing out the discipline like this. "I will always be here, Sheridan. I'll be here Christmas and spring break. And every holiday weekend. Or, hell—I'll go there. I've always wanted to see California. The point is, I'm gonna wait for you. You already know there's no one else for me. My wolf would never accept another mate. He picked you. You're it." The whole time I bare my soul to her, I'm spanking away.

I'm not worried about hurting her, because shifters heal instantly, so my only worry is pissing her off, and she doesn't seem pissed.

I stop spanking and squeeze her ass.

"More," she moans.

Fuck *me.*

As you wish, sweetheart.

I unbutton her shorts and yank them off, along with her panties, dropping to a crouch to help her untangle them from her legs. After I stand, I pepper her ass with slaps, varying my target so she never knows where the next one will fall—one time on the back of her thigh, the next on her other cheek, then her pussy. I slap until her ass turns rosy red and her pussy grows slick and swollen.

Then I pick up a pen and shove it between her fingers. "Fill out the acceptance letter."

"No. I'm not ready to make that decision."

I shove back the heaviness that threatens to descend. Believe me, I get it. Living apart from Sheridan would be the worst kind of suckage ever. But we're talking *Stanford.*

"Fill it out. Send it in. You can always change your mind later." *Not that I'll let you.*

She gives an exaggerated sigh, still refusing to hold the pen I was pressing her fingers around.

I glance around the desk and snatch up a ruler from her pen jar.

"Fill it out, baby, or you're going to get paddled."

She laughs in my face. "Please. That won't do much."

She's right. It was a thin little piece of wood. If I used it hard enough, it would probably break. Still, I take her words as a challenge and apply the ruler thoroughly, first to one cheek, then the other.

She squeals and shifts on her feet—I think it works. The ruler leaves cute red stripes. Too bad they'll heal so fast—I rather like the idea of leaving marks on her. Something to remember me by.

"Fill it out."

She laughs. "Okay, okay. I'm filling it out."

I rub her reddened ass, squeezing roughly. My dick is so hard it's going to break off and I already know this scene is going to be in my spank bank for years to come.

I pull a condom out of my pocket and rip it open while Sheridan checks the box and signs her name.

I pop her on the ass again twice, once on each cheek. "Put it in the envelope."

She giggles and does as she's told. I fucking love that she trusts me enough to let me dominate her this way, that she's as turned on by it as I am.

I spring my erection and roll the condom on. "Now for your fucking," I say, like it's a punishment, too.

She hollows her back, lifts her blushing ass to me. Hell to the yeah. I push in, slow at first, but she's plenty wet, totally ready.

Okay, then.

She's going to get it hard.

"Keeping secrets from me has consequences," I say, pushing her torso down further, until she's flat against the desk. I press my hand to the back of her neck to hold her in place.

"Oh yeah? What are they?" Her husky voice nearly makes me jizz in the condom right there.

"You're about to find out, sweetheart." I grip her nape and use my hold to leverage myself back and into her again, slamming hard.

She grunts, then moans.

"You're going to take it hard today, little wolf. I'm going to fuck you until you can't walk."

She lets out a sweet little whimper and I continue to ram into her, slapping my loins against her hot ass, shoving her feet wider.

"Are you going to keep things from me again, baby?"

"Ugn, no," she moans.

I piston faster. "That's right. You're not. Because now you know what happens."

I'm feeling like a porn star, the kind who uses and degrades his partner in the worst kind of the way, but I can't find it in me to feel bad, because Sheridan is loving the hell out of it. In fact, it's hard to tell who's getting off more—we're both about to blow so hard the roof flies off the house.

Her sounds grow more urgent, cries more needy and stars dance behind my eyelids.

My thighs shake, balls draw up right. "Fuck, Sheridan, fuck!" I can't stop the urge to fuck her harder, drill deeper, so deep she'll remember me every time she moves.

"Please, Trey," she moans.

"I'm going to come," I warn, because there's no holding it back now.

"Yes, come!"

I slam into her and shoot my load, and she shrieks, body convulsing beneath mine. I pull her torso up until her back meets my chest and pinch both her nipples while we both still come and come straight into tomorrow.

Like always before I shift, my vision domes, canines lengthen. If I don't mark her soon, I'll go fucking moon mad. But I hold strong for her. She's too young. Her dad would kill me. I'll wait until the time is right and we both agree. I grit my teeth and hold my wolf at bay, my muscles shaking with the effort.

When I have control, I squeeze her firm breasts and stroke my cock in and out. "That's it, sweetheart. There's no getting away from me. You could go to college across the Earth and I'd still wait for you. Or I'd come find you when you were done. You're mine."

"Mark me," she whispers.

Fuck! My teeth descend further.

"Not yet," I grit and pull out, not trusting myself to keep touching her when she's tempting me so fucking hard.

"Why not?" She turns to challenge me.

I step back. "You need to be sure. Once I claim you, there's no backing out."

She pulls the collar of her t-shirt down to offer her shoulder for my bite.

"Baby," I croak. I'm fucking dying here. My cock's gone rock hard again, serum coats my teeth, ready to be embedded into her skin, to claim her as mine forever.

But this is just like the college thing. I'm not going to let her screw her future out of some eighteen-year-old's impulse to mate the first guy she fucks.

"We'll talk about it later." I turn away from her, as if removing the sight of her beautiful face will somehow tamp down the wolf's raging desire.

"I love you, Trey," she says softly to my back.

I almost drop to my knees.

How this girl can simultaneously make me into a man and humble me is beyond me.

I whirl and throw her over my shoulder, carrying her to the bed. I have to claim her again. I'm not giving her my bite, but I sure as hell can't keep my cock away from her.

Present

SHERIDAN

THE VAMPIRES' club is tucked in El Mercado district, near the trolley stop, at the edge of their territory. A nondescript stucco building with nice landscaping and a pretty stone walkway. I'm there right at dusk, and sit in my car with the top up, watching the sun melt below the horizon in a storm of color.

The only thing to fear is fear itself. I tap my dashboard with my finger, readying myself to walk into the vampires' stronghold. The fact that Lucius the leech king gave the invitation doesn't reassure me at all. Vampires love their invitations—and they don't need permission to get inside a victim's head. Lucius wouldn't have extended one if he wasn't sure he held the upper hand. He's up to something. Maybe it has to do with the mysterious black car I keep glimpsing on my block.

Someone knocks on my window and I jolt in my seat with a squawk until I meet Trey's baby blues, my alarm reflected in their depths.

Trey gives me a concerned look as I roll down my window. "Everything okay?"

"Yeah. Just, you know, nervous." I don't mention the mysterious black car sitting outside my house a couple times this week. After the story of my stalker, he might not take it well.

Trey opens my door and I hop out. He's dressed in his usual biker guy outfit: another leather jacket, white shirt and black jeans with his wallet on a chain. His hair is spiked with fresh gel, and his boots slightly less dusty and scuffed than usual.

He's scowling at me.

"What?" I look down at my chest. " Do I have something on my shirt?"

"That's not a shirt."

"You're right." I fiddle with the zipper between my girls, tugging it down another millimeter before twirling on my Louboutins to give him the entire view. "I think technically it's called a catsuit." I smooth my hands down the sharp angle from my waist to my flaring hips, and strike a pose. "Meow."

"Fuck," Trey mutters. "Where do you get these outfits, anyway?"

"BDSM-R-Us." I lean into him, inhaling his scent, a masculine mix of aftershave and motor oil. His arms go around me automatically. I can't stop myself from wriggling closer. "Is that a lead pipe in your jeans or are you happy to see me?"

"Fuck me." He holds me close, burying his face in my hair, and I'd wager he's enjoying the mingle of our scents. I know I am.

"I got you something to wear," I murmur.

"Oh yeah?" His breath wafts over my ear as he nuzzles my neck.

I step back and he lets me go, following me with a hungry gaze.

Then he sees what I pull out of the store bag. "Fuck

no!" He jumps back as if I've Tazed him.

I hold up the leash and silver-studded collar. "No? It'll go with your outfit," I singsong, strutting on my heels as he backs away. "Actually, no. You need to be naked." His groan deepens as I wave the bag at him, enjoying the results of my gag gift. "You don't want to be my little doggie?"

"Really fucking funny."

"That's *No, mistress*," I instruct with a smug smile.

With a growl, Trey advances. I back up, wide-eyed, as all six feet of him comes at me, horn-gry and looking like an avenging biker god. He snatches the leash and collar from my hand. "I'll take this."

"You're gonna wear it?" My mouth drops open a little. I only got it as a joke.

He shoots me a look of pure menacing promise. "One of us is gonna wear it tonight. But it's not going to be me." He pretends to inspect the leather goods. The wickedness in his eyes sends zings straight to inner thighs. My knees wobble.

I may have pushed the wolf too far.

Trapping my gaze in ice, he pulls the store bag from my hand. "What else you got?"

"A-a, um, gag gift," I stutter. "Literally."

He holds up the red ball gag. "Nice." He turns it over before pocketing it, along with the leash and collar. "Should come in handy."

He catches my elbow right before my legs give out. "Let's go."

The last of the sun's rays dive behind the mountains as we walk up to the club. A pale human greets us at the door, a black strip of ribbon tied around his neck. He's thin and anemic, but good-looking in a boy band sort of way.

"Welcome to Club Toxic."

I take my last breath of fresh air, the hair on the back of my neck prickling at the vampires' scent as I step into their lair.

The doorman offers to take our jackets and I give him a toothy grin. "I don't have one."

Trey folds his arms over his chest, his glower a clear refusal. The human doesn't balk—doesn't show any expression really. I check his neck for bite marks but can't see anything under the satin choker that seems to be a makeshift collar. Probably why he's wearing it.

"We're early," Trey murmurs, looking around the empty dance floor. A few people sit in booths or stand at tall tables, but there's barely anyone here.

"On purpose. I wanted to stake out our territory before a crowd shows up." As we walk across the room, I stay as close to him as I can without actually leaning on him. He doesn't seem to mind. The scent of vampires clogs my nose.

Trey takes a derisive sniff. "Smells like a dish drain."

I almost laugh at that—the empty, earthy scent reminds me of a drain pipe, or a root cellar. Or a tomb.

The bartender—another human with a blank face and satin choker—pours us drinks without commenting on how early we are.

"Can you let Frangelico know we're here?" I ask our guide. The pasty human blinks at us but nods and disappears into the back. "Did you see any fang marks on him?" I ask Trey in a whisper.

"No. But he could be a junkie. He smells wrong."

Trey picks up his drink but doesn't taste it. His gaze sweeps the room like a guard on the the lookout. "So this is a vampire club? Kinda boring."

"We're hours early."

"You think Frangelico will meet with us?"

"Maybe. Or send one of his lieutenants. Julius Caesar or whatever."

"Oh yeah." Trey shakes his head. A group of people enter the club, and he straightens. We both fall silent, scanning each figure. They're all thin and beautiful and plastic-looking, but none of them are vampires.

We stand in the corner for over an hour, pretending to nurse our drinks without actually touching them, and watch the place fill. At some point a DJ shows up and starts blasting the latest popular dance tunes. The floor swells with bodies bumping and grinding. "The leeches aren't having any problem making this place popular," Trey murmurs in my ear so I can hear him over the sinful beat.

"I wonder if any of them sense they're prey," I muse, my eyes following one particularly beautiful redhead. She's freckled and curvy, with a sweetness I haven't seen in any of the jaded crowd. A dark clad form slips out from the shadows, taking her hand and bowing over it. From my vantage point, I can't see the man's face, but the redhead looks up at him with an expression of awe tinged with lust. The tall man tucks her hand under his arm and guides her back towards the door, only to detour and disappear behind the coat check area.

"Trey." I nudge him. "I think I know where the real action is."

He follows my eyes. "Gotcha. Lead the way. I got your back."

We set our drinks down and mosey across the dance floor. The crowd parts for us.

The human at the door doesn't seem surprised to see us. "He's expecting you," he says politely, stepping aside to reveal a few steps leading down to another door, painted black to match the walls. The door yawns open, revealing a long set of stairs leading to some sort of basement.

I hide my disgust—how long was he going to let us wait before fetching us to the real Toxic, the club beneath the club?

"Stupid leeches, always playing games," Trey mutters exactly what I'm thinking. His large hand on my back steadies me as we descend into the shadowy depths. The dark walls shake with the deep bass of the music above us. When we reach the bottom of the steps, we pause a second to let our eyes adjust. A purple neon tube runs around the room near the ceiling, shedding an eerie light. Dark shapes and monoliths loom out of the shadows.

Ahead, the pale skin of the redhead shines like a beacon. She's like a wraith led by a black-clad emissary, summoning her to Hades. The suit holding her hands turns and I gasp as I recognize the vampire's beautiful features. Nero smirks at me before guiding his human prey to a piece of heavy wooden furniture topped with shiny leather. A spanking bench.

"Fuck me," Trey mutters, looking around the room. "Is this what you were expecting?"

"Yep," I whisper. "Are you ready to use that collar?"

"Only if you're gonna wear it," he tells me. I bite my lip to hide the thrill singing through me. I seem to remember Trey has more than a bit of sexual dominance in him, ready to come out. Even as a teenager, he knew just what to do. The glint in his eyes tells me he sees my suppressed excitement.

More people come down the stairs, and we step aside to let them pass. Vampires ooze from the shadows of the dungeon, claiming their humans and leading them away. Throughout the room, tops start tying up bottoms, cuffing them or chaining them to the wall or available spanking horses and tables. The club music is broken by the sound of whips snapping, and the plaintive cries of the eager victims. None of the vampires are playing the role of submissive.

"This is nuts," Trey comments, but his voice is deeper, thicker. I nod, glad no one can see how tight my nipples are, how hot and flushed my lower belly feels.

"Welcome, wolves," a smooth voice behind us has us whirling, and lips curled back in a half snarl. Lucius the leech king stands in a spotlit corner, posing in front of a giant portrait of himself. He looks like freaking Dorian Gray, wearing the same sinful smile and red velvet robe as his painted image.

"Hello," I say before Trey can growl or bark or insult our host. "Thank you for inviting us in."

"You are always welcome here, my dear," he purrs, like

the lecherous villain in a bad movie. The only thing he's missing is a pipe and Playboy twins.

The vampire king glides forward and I have to force myself not to step back. At my side, Trey growls. Lucius moves just another inch closer to me and stops, making it clear that he's not intimidated by Trey. "You asked me about sweetblood."

"Yes." I stare at the lapel of his velvet robe.

"It is not a drug, although we vampires find it intoxicating. Look there."

We follow his pointing to the wall, where a vampire in black slacks and shirt sleeves—his sleeves rolled up to present taut forearms, flogs a wilting woman. The leather strands snap and fall, followed by moans. She doesn't sound like she's in pain.

"There is a certain type of person who enjoys pain, yes?" The vampire's voice echoes right in my ear, sounding like he's standing much closer than he is. "The body has ways of rewarding such stoicism."

"Endorphins," I agree. My thoughts feel sluggish. Older vampires can control with just their voice. My hand fumbles at my side, finding Trey's, I squeeze his fingers tight. He squeezes me back and my mind clears.

"Yes. For such a reward, some people crave the pain. You call them masochists." Lucius nods at the woman at the wall. Her vampire top has switched out the flogger for a longer, evil-looking whip. I can smell her arousal from here. "We call them sweetbloods." His voice drops to a haunted whisper. "The pain makes the blood sweeter."

After a snap of the single tail, the woman droops in her

bonds. The vampire glides to her side, and runs a hand down the fresh red marks on her side. The submissive shudders and the vampire steps close, murmuring softly. He unhooks the cuffs and supports her sagging body. With one arm he holds her up as the other brushes the hair back from her face and neck and draws her close. The light glints off his fangs.

I gasp and turn towards Trey, breathing hard.

"Sheridan," Trey's voice is blast of fresh air, sweet and bracing. His arms slide around me, holding me up like the vampire held his victim. "You all right?"

I nod, tipping my head back so he can see my expression. His worried look clears. "You like it."

I nod, and he touches my face in wonder.

Lucius' laugh echoes around us. "I will leave you to explore my little club. Enjoy."

I don't turn to watch him leave, but I know the moment he's gone. The vampire/victim couple has also disappeared, maybe into one of the curtained alcoves that line the room.

Trey still holds me close. "If this is too much, we can go." His chest rumbles under my ear.

"I'm all right." I give him another squeeze. He's so warm and strong, a living rock.

"You sure?"

"I'm all right," I repeat. "I want to stay."

His gaze searches my face, and I flinch away. I don't want him to see this side of me, raw and vulnerable. I push away from him, but he keeps his arms locked around me.

"You can go if you want to," I mutter, and his gaze turns cold.

"I'm staying."

"You sure?" I mimic his question from a moment before. I'm mocking him because I don't want him looking too closely. I don't want him to see how much all this stuff turns me on.

The expression on his face tells me he already knows.

"Trey, let go of me," I whisper.

"You sure?" He's not mocking me. His thumb brushes over my knuckles, and I realize I'm hanging onto him, tight.

Oops.

When I step away from Trey, I find Nero standing close, too close to me.

"Hello, little wolf," he says and I stiffen. Trey's arm slides around my waist, but I step away from him before he can pull me back into his chest. It's time I face the vampires on my own two feet.

What doesn't kill me...

"I'm not afraid of you," I blurt, raising my chin in the air.

"Of course not. I can smell you from here. You smell...good." He makes it sound obscene. "You like this place."

"It's growing on me," I answer.

"There is much to enjoy." Nero grins, showing fang. There's no sign of the redhead he came down here with. I wonder if she's in an alcove, resting, a glass of orange juice and bar of chocolate waiting nearby. Aftercare for a BDSM scene or a vampire feed?

Nero runs his hand over the leather padding of a

raised bench. "I will be your guide, if you wish it. Virgil to your Dante."

"*Abandon all hope, ye who enter here?*" I quote Dante's *Inferno* and the vampire's grin widens.

"Exactly. Are you ready to come with me?"

Before I can answer, Trey growls. "Over my dead body." Trey steps between me and the vampire. "Do you want this?"

I freeze when he holds up the collar. "Do you want to try this? Scene here?"

"Trey," I whisper.

"Sheridan." His tone warns me not to play. "Tell me."

"Yes." Yes, I want to try this. "But not with you." Not after last night. I'm way too raw to offer myself up to him again only to be led to my car and told goodnight. No, it's better not to get sexually involved with Trey. More sexually involved, that is.

"Not an option," he growls and backs me to the wall, blocking me from anyone who might approach. "What's your safeword, sweetheart?"

I lick my lips. Crap. My body is already surrendering. It already knows its master. "Spreadsheet." I'm a finance major and an MBA, and I take accounting seriously. Any talk of work will pretty much kill the mood.

He shakes his head, smirking in a way that I know means he gets the joke. I draw back as he gets close, but after a moment lift my hair and let him buckle on the collar. Trey runs a gentle finger around my neck to check the fit and I'm helpless, legs turning to liquid, core molten, lips parting to welcome his as I stare into his eyes.

"Perfect," he murmurs, and dips his head close enough

to whisper in my ear. "You didn't buy this collar for me, did you?"

Swallowing, I shake my head. He leads me forward, then turns and backs me into a sturdy frame. The wooden limbs of a Saint Andrew's cross spread over my head, a heavy piece with silver studs and leather padding, and cuffs dangling at ankle and wrist height.

Trey secures one arm, then the other, and kneels to tie my legs. Beyond him, Nero watches, his face in shadow.

When Trey rises, my stomach flip-flops at the aura of command enveloping him. Like he flipped a switch, and instead of moonbrained biker dude, I have Trey The Dominant, ready to Rock. My. World.

"Trey, wait," I say as he reexamines the cuff.

He pinches my fingertips, checking my circulation. "You feel okay?"

"Yes." I squirm. I have dreams of being tied up like this, but I don't want Trey doing it. I mean, I've fantasized about him doing it, but now that's happening, I want it to stop. Don't I?

"Wait a second," I beg as he checks my other hand. "Let's stop and talk about this."

Trey hesitates, frowning. "You want to stop, give me your safeword."

The word *spreadsheet* rests on the tip of my tongue. I just have to say it, and I'll be free. I can leave Trey and the club behind, go home and get myself off to the memory of this for the rest of my life. That's what I want to do, right?

After a long silence, Trey murmurs, "Yeah, I thought so. Say your safeword and this stops. Otherwise, we're doing this. You want this. I know you do."

"Let me go," I hiss.

He shakes his head slowly. "No way, sweetheart. Not when I have you right where I want you."

∾

Trey

I DON'T HAVE my own implements. I notice the other doms are carrying duffel bags with equipment, so I make do. I pull my leather belt from the loops and wind the buckle end around my fist.

Sheridan stares with wide eyes, half-nervous, half-thrilled. My wolf is actually calmer than I would expect—it's like he senses the danger here, knows I need to keep my head.

Thank fuck, because her scent is driving me wild.

Sheridan looks sexy as hell in her skin-tight leather outfit, and as much as I'd love to watch her skin turn pink under my leather belt, there's no way I'm going to let any asshole here see her naked. I sort of like the idea of her having the layer of protection, anyway. I would die if I actually hurt her.

I wind the belt until less than a foot remains and then step in front of her. Her glorious tits rise and fall as she pants, irises changed from green to amber. "Beautiful wolf," I murmur and slap the belt across the front of her thigh. She jerks, but smiles.

"Again."

I run my thumb over her lower lip. She nips at it.

"Cute, sweetheart, but you're not in charge. I'm the one giving the orders tonight."

Her eyes dilate and she tosses her beautiful head. I stand back to survey her with an exaggeratedly thoughtful expression, then smack the belt right up between her legs.

She squeals, her body going rigid against the cross, then sagging. Her belly trembles on her exhale.

I slap her inner thigh, several times, then move to the other side.

The little sounds she makes nearly kill me. I'm getting dizzy and drugged myself, which isn't good.

Keep your head. Stay cool.

I want to tear open that sexy catsuit and fuck her right against the cross. And you'd better fucking believe I bought condoms today. I lunge into her, squeezing her breasts roughly as I claim her mouth.

She moans against my lips, nipping and licking like she's frantic for more.

I back up, depriving her of the satisfaction she craves.

Another slap between the legs. The sound of the leather smacking leather is delicious. I whip her pussy again, and again.

"Harder," she moans. She appears completely drugged. I can see how a woman in this state might taste different to a blood-sucker. She's definitely high. But I swear to the fates, if any of them come near this wolf, I will kill them all, and start the war to end all wars.

Out of the corner of my eye, I see Nero hanging around, watching the scene. I bare my teeth and growl, warning him back, but he merely throws back his head and laughs.

"Trey," Sheridan mewls. Need drips in her voice.

"Not yet, baby. I'm not done whipping your front side yet. And when I finish, I have to turn you around and warm your ass. You're lucky you're wearing that catsuit and I'm too fucking possessive to let anyone see you without its protection."

She licks her lips, her glassy gaze tracking my face. "And then?"

I give her a toothy grin. "Then, I'll think about letting you come."

She growls and fights the restraints, some of her submission ebbing. I laugh and slap up each of her inner thighs again.

I smack her pussy. "You want more of my belt here, little wolf?"

She rolls her head from side to side, chest heaving. "Yes! Fuck, Trey."

My eyes bug out of my head. "Holy shit! You said it."

She leans forward, straining at the bonds. "I said it. Now you do it."

I laugh in total wonder, reward her with a hard, demanding kiss. I cup her mons with my free hand, apply firm pressure in undulations.

Her breaths grow even shorter, quicker. "Please, Trey."

"And to think, all you needed was a little sexual stimulation."

She tries to nip my lips. "Stop teasing. I need it."

I arch a brow. "Need what, beautiful?"

"This. More. You," she moans. "I need it all. Please, Trey."

I reach up and release her wrists, then her ankles. I

turn her on the cross and press her face first against the padded front. I replace the restraints and she waggles her hips, like she's trying to get relief by rubbing against the cross. It's damn near the hottest thing I've ever seen.

"Naughty girl," I scold and whip her across the ass. I can tell she loves it because she hollows her back and sticks her butt out for more.

I let out a little more slack in the belt and whip her again and again, concentrating on the lower half of her ass, then working down each individual thigh.

Her moans grow louder and faster, like she's going to come just from being whipped. My cock surges against my jeans. My vision starts to dome and my teeth lengthen, ready to mark her. Fuck, I may not get through this.

I glance over at the leech in the shadows again to regain my head. It helps. I draw a slow inhale in through my nostrils and keep steadily whipping Sheridan's ass, when her cries reach a desperate pitch, I whip between her legs.

She chokes on a breath.

I whip again.

A keening mewl.

Another thwap against her clit.

She shrieks and her muscles seize up, a glorious shuddering running through her luscious form.

"That's it, baby." I drop the belt and slap with my hand —only because I need to get close to her—need to feel those muscles squeezing as she comes from her pussy whipping. I slap and slap—light, quick smacks until she tumbles down the other side of her release and goes limp, sagging into her bonds.

The moment I see it, I work her free of the bonds and wrap my leather jacket around her shoulders. "That's it, baby. You were so beautiful." I swing her up into my arms, ignoring the hungry stares of the leeches around us.

I don't give a shit about pack-vampire relations or our mission to spy right now. I just need to get Sheridan out of there. Take her home and put her to bed.

Naked.

With me on top.

~

Sheridan

I'm drunk on endorphins for the entire ride home—I hardly notice that Trey's put me in the passenger side of my car and took my keys to drive. When we get out, I throw my head back, like I'm in wolf form and am going to howl at the moon.

The moon bathes me in her beauty—she's full and lush, her feminine power amplifying mine.

Trey's eyes glint silver, too, and I suddenly can't believe he's never marked me. Our wolves were made for each other. How could we have denied it all these years? I lunge at him, twisting his shirt up in my fingers, smashing my lips over his.

He stumbles back, a surprised chuckle puffing between us, then yanks me up to straddle his waist. I bite his neck, lick his ear, rub my breasts against his chest. Somehow, he gets us inside and then we tear at each other's clothes. I shred his shirt. He yanks my catsuit off me. His jeans and boxer briefs come off.

My skin is still warm and tingly from the whipping he gave me back at Toxic, the pulse between my legs insistent. He advances, tall, naked, potent. Tattoos curl around his forearms, over his shoulders and across his chest. His cock stands out, huge and erect.

I reach for his cock. It's been a long time since I've had sex—twelve years, to be exact—but my body remembers. My body knows.

Trey catches my wrist before I can grasp his length. With his other hand, he fists my hair and tugs my head back. "Careful, baby," he rumbles, bringing his lips to my jaw. "You get me too excited, and it will all be over before we start."

I give a shaky laugh. Trey shifts to hold me around the waist and he walks with me to the bed, tumbles me down with him on top.

I can't wait. I don't want to go slow. I pull him to me, over me, my nails sinking into his back. His cock prods my entrance and I rock my hips, trying to help him in.

"Wait...hang on," Trey chokes. He backs off me and retrieves a condom from the pocket of his jeans. I pinch my nipples and toss my legs around on the bed while I wait, which pulls a distinctly animal-like snarl from his lips. He rips the foil open with his teeth.

Will he mark me?

I can't even think it, and yet goosebumps race over my skin as I watch his canines lengthen, the silver glow of his wolf eyes. On some level, I know this is it—he won't hold back.

I've tried his self-control too many times.

He sheaths his cock and I climb up on my knees to meet him, but he pushes me back. He holds his thumb over my neck, not choking me, but holding me down.

Showing me who's in charge.

My knees spread wide and I take him into the cradle of my legs. He rubs the head of his cock over my slit and I arch up, sucking in a shaky breath. I'm so freaking sensitive right now, I swear to the fates I could come again, just from him *talking* to my clit.

He pushes at my sopping entrance, stretching me as I take the head in. I draw in a sharp breath when he spears me in a single thrust and he freezes.

"Were you ready, baby?" His concern nearly makes me weep. He's the same tender, thoughtful man he was twelve years ago when he first took my virginity.

I grab his ass and hold him in as I get used to his size. "Yeah, I pant. It's just been awhile."

Understatement.

My eyes slide to the side but when I sneak a peek back at his face, he's staring down at me with an intensity I can't look away from. I rock my pelvis up to move him inside me.

"There's never been another for me." His voice is rough and deep. He holds my gaze as he eases out and slams back in.

I gasp at the intensity of it—both his words and his thrust. "You mean...you never *loved* anyone else?" I'm trying to make sense of what he's trying to tell me. He can't be talking about sex, right? No male stays celibate for twelve years.

His upper lip twitches in a snarl as he jacks back and in again, stealing my breath. "Loved. Fucked. Dated. *Only you.*"

It's ridiculous, but uncontrollable. I burst into tears.

Because... *Trey.*

My Trey.

He's still mine. Never wasn't mine.

"What about—" I don't want to, but I have to ask.

He gives a quick shake of his head, changes his rhythm to short, hard thrusts. "I had to. To make you leave. You were supposed to go to college. Make something of your life."

I'm fully sobbing now, and yet somehow still completely in sync with the sex, still needy for it, turned on by it.

"I've never been with anyone else, either," I confess on a sob. I match the rocking of my hips with his thrusts, take him deeper. "It was only you for me, too."

"Fuck," Trey curses, closing his eyes, the veins standing out on his neck as he hammers into me faster, harder. "Fuck, Sheridan. I'm sorry. I never wanted to hurt you."

"I'm sorry I hurt you, too. I was such a bitch."

Time slows. Rearranges. Or else we enter into no-time. All I know is the delicious slide and smack of his thrusts, the sensation of being filled and emptied, and all the while deeply held, revered, honored.

There's magic sparking between us. Our wolves are meeting on the same level as our human selves—perfectly matched, perfectly in tune.

And then he roars, bucking so hard my butt bounces

off the bed with each rebound, ramming the bed into the wall.

There's a snarl and a sharp, satisfying pain.

The scent of my blood mingled with the scent of his essence. My arousal. Sex.

Marking.

Love.

The scent of love.

He falls down onto me and I sob into his neck—happy, glorious sobs.

He claimed me. He never meant to hurt me.

I'm finally where I belong. Where we belong.

Together.

Prese

CHAPTER TEN

PRESENT

I'VE NEVER WOKEN up with a man before. It's delicious. Trey's warm limbs are curled around me, his scent fills my nostrils. I turn into his embrace and nuzzle his neck. Then I remember that he marked me, and touch my own.

The wounds have already closed. I run my finger over the raised areas. Trey tangles his fingers over mine and traces the marks with his thumb. "Tell me it wasn't a mistake." Worry glints in his gaze.

He always was a thinker.

An *over*-thinker, when it came to me.

He let me hate him just to make sure I'd go to Stanford!

Sweet, infuriating male.

But my mouth goes dry when I think—really think—

about what this means. My parents will flip. One of us will have to move. We barely have a relationship to stand on. Yeah, maybe he jumped the gun.

If by jumping the gun I mean holding off for twelve years.

"Not a mistake," I say, though. Because I can't believe it was. I won't. There's no way the two of us would each wait twelve years for someone who hated us if it wasn't meant to be.

He leans his forehead against mine.

"It doesn't change things. I wore your mark already—on my heart."

Trey relaxes. "I wore yours, too." He taps his chest. We're quiet a moment, his hand smoothing over my bare skin, up my hip and back down again.

"I can't believe the outfit you wore last night," he says out of nowhere. "Or, shit, the one you wore at the fight."

"Oh yeah?" I prop myself up. "You like my little costumes?"

"Are they that, though? Costumes?" His eyes pierce mine.

I blink. "Well, yeah. I mean, it's not like that's what I wear to work."

He just stares at me and I swallow. Of course Trey sees too much. Right through my lies, straight into my soul. After a long silence, I swallow. "All those outfits are just for fun. They're not the real me."

"Aren't they?"

"No." I frown, looking away, and he lays a hand on my cheek, guiding me back to face him. "They're just for fun," I whisper.

He presses his lips together, blows out a breath, and then it's his turn to look away. Right at my closet, as if he has x-ray vision and can pick out all the freaky costumes I'm hiding in there.

"What?" I ask.

"I see things differently. The suits you wear, the daddy's girl act—I think that's the costume. Maybe the nights you let down your hair, that's the real you."

I lay down on my back, grabbing my pillow. I want to cover my face. "I don't think so."

Trey hasn't moved. He's still propped up, gazing down at me. Only now, his eyes turn tender. "I do."

I roll away, bringing the pillow up to muffle my words. "Whatever."

His palm smacks down on my left butt cheek.

I roll back, snarling. "Hey!"

He laughs and grips my bottom hard for a moment, before giving it a deep massage. "You can't hide from me."

"I'm not hiding," I pout.

"Not from me. Never from me." He raises a blond brow. "I know all your secrets." Dropping his head, he gives my shoulder a kiss. "They"—his lips trespass to the vulnerable spot under my ear—"are"—he catches my earlobe between his teeth and tugs—"all"—he pretends to gnaw on the outer rim of my ear. My eyes flutter closed. My ears are so sensitive—"mine."

His tongue thrusts in, and sensation shoots straight through me, detonating between my legs. I try to twist away from him and his hands grip me harder, holding me down and helpless. I writhe against the sheets, growing hotter for him by the second.

He crawls lower and spreads my thighs, rolling my knees back to my shoulders. One long lap, and he has me straining against his hold. Shivering for more.

"Trey," I rasp.

"You taste so good, baby." He smacks his lips and dives down for more, licking into me, swirling his tongue between my labia, up around my clit.

I moan and wiggle and push my knees into his hands, but he continues his torture, flicking his tongue over my clit, then suctioning his lips over it to suck. Just when I'm about to go off, he stops and backs off me. "Roll over."

It's on the tip of my lips to demand why, or give him crap, but I remember how much I loved his domination last night, and do what he asks. Instantly I'm transformed to a slightly giggly, trembling bundle of anticipation. I hear the rip of a condom and Trey climbs over me, nudging my legs apart.

"I have twelve years to make up for," Trey growls, like it's going to be a punishment and impales me. He's still too big, but I'm a shifter, so I'm not sore and I freaking love the position. Trey's loins push against my ass, the head of his cock hits a spot inside me that makes me moan.

I tangle my fingers in the sheets, grip hard to hang on as he picks up his pace, dipping deeper each time.

"Trey—fates—Trey," I moan.

He curses and picks up speed, smacking my ass with his loins, screwing me harder and harder.

Despite holding onto the sheets, he propels me to the top of the bed, where I brace my arms against the headboard.

"Oh that's, hot, baby." Trey pulls out and lifts my hips, so I'm up on my knees with my chest pressed against the bed. He enters me in this position, and I'm instantly moaning, totally ready to come.

Apparently, it's good for him, too, because his fingers dig into my hips, breaths turn into snarls.

"Sheridan—fuck!" He reaches around the front of me and slaps my clit.

I come on a scream. He roars and flattens me to the bed, coming and coming with wild, pulsing thrusts. He kisses my neck, rocks against my ass slowly, tenderly. "How could I have let you go?" he murmurs.

My heart squeezes. I haven't fully forgiven him for it, even though I understand.

He gets up to dispose of the condom and I roll over. My stomach growls, loudly and I clap a hand over it and giggle.

"Gotta feed my baby." He plants a soft one on my lips.

"I love a man who cooks." He strides off, the play of his muscles in his back mesmerizing.

It hits me. I don't have to hide from Trey. He likes me for me.

I climb out of bed and throw on a pair of panties.

So he likes my wild outfits? Might as well bless him with another one.

I stand in the closet, designing a new outfit I'm going to call "Sheridan up front, slutty in the back", when a weird beeping noise pulls me away from trying to figure out what cardigan to wear over cut off shorts and a crop top. I hunt under the blankets and find the ringing mobile —Trey's—just as he swaggers back in.

"Food's ready."

"Great." I hand him the phone. It cuts out ringing just to start ringing again. "Someone's popular. This early, you'd think they'd leave a voicemail."

He frowns at the screen. "It's Grizz. Hang on." Bars of light from the blinds rest on his face as he takes the call. I curl around a pillow, trying not to eavesdrop.

"Yeah." His shoulders stiffen, every line in his body alert and haunted. He turns away, as if protecting me from whoever's on the line. "No. Got it."

"What's wrong?" I reach out my hand and he flinches away. Close enough to touch, but so far away.

"I gotta go," Trey says. "There's a dead body at Fight Club."

All the oxygen sucks from the room. "Shifter?"

"No." Trey's blue eyes are bleak. "Human."

WHEN WE PULL up to the club, Grizz is standing guard, his scarred face still as stone. He's a life-sized gargoyle until we approach and he moves to intercept us. "Boss."

"Where's the body?" Trey asks grimly.

Grizz brings us to the back door. The body is a limp pile half-leaning against the door, soft red hair spilling over the face. I bite my fist to stifle a cry. The redhead at the club—could it be her? Did she scene with a vampire and disappear, a victim to Nero's bloodlust? Did he whip her flesh in a frenzy and drag her to an alcove to drain her dry because he was angry with me?

Did I cause this?

Then Trey stoops down, brushing the hair aside. It's not a woman, but a young man with matching red hair. That doesn't help any. It could've been her.

I close my eyes, breathing deep to steady myself. My nose fills with the scent of the dead. Underneath the corpse smell is a subtle cologne that doesn't quite cover the cold scent of a vampire.

"Fang marks on the neck," Trey confirms. Trey looks ten years older as he handles the body, his large, calloused hands infinitely gentle. "Already stiff. Rigor mortis setting in."

"Must've waited 'til dawn to dump him," Grizz says. "I kicked everyone out around two thirty. Left an hour later, figuring I'd finish clean up this morning. If they were monitoring this place, they know I rise early and get back here before eight, even after fight nights. They had a two, maybe three hour window."

"Do you have cameras?" I ask, fear and bile still clogging my throat.

"No." Both shake their heads.

"We don't need 'em," Grizz mutters. "We know who did this." *Vampires.*

"We need to know which one," I protest. "Frangelico seemed to think his nest knew how to eat without killing. He might not have sanctioned this."

Grizz shakes his head. "Only good vampire is a dead one," he growls, before giving me his back.

I jolt as a motorcycle roars up into the club lot, spraying gravel. Jared dismounts and strides to us. The closer he gets, the more his expression grows more shadowed. He crouches in front of the body, raising his nose to the air. One sniff is all he needs.

"Fuck," he explodes up, pacing away while raking a hand through his hair.

Trey's big hands pull me close. I lean into him and shiver, even though it's not cold. "You all right?" he murmurs.

"I'll be fine," I answer, as Jared paces back.

"This is fucking bullshit," he barks. "Fucking vamps, playing games. I knew we shouldn't have trusted them."

"We don't know if it was Frangelico," I caution.

"Of course it is," Jared explodes. "He reeled us in to agree to a treaty, and pulls this shit to prove how all powerful he is."

I want to argue that it could be a rogue vampire acting against Frangelico, but bite my lip. Now isn't the time.

A growl rumbles in Trey's chest and I splay a hand over his heart, facing Jared. "Doesn't matter who did it. We need to act. Cops will ask questions if they find the body."

"We gotta move it," Jared says.

"I can do it," Grizz says. "I have my truck."

"I'll help," Trey squeezes me before breaking away.

"Wait. You hear that?" Jared asks. We all cock our ears. Trey starts swearing and doesn't stop as the piercing emergency sirens grow louder and louder.

Trey

I STAND in the middle of the fight club lot, my hands loose and open at my sides. Best not to make fists and look angry with this many cops around. Staying relaxed is a real effort.

Behind me, the officers question Grizz and Jared. They already interviewed Sheridan and me. I called Garrett to get his mate Amber, a lawyer, down here in case they find a reason to haul us away. Of all of us, they're the most suspicious of Grizz, shooting him dark looks and muttering. The bear is the most likely suspect—he's from out of state, found the body, and has priors.

Someone fucking set us up. The tip was phoned in at 8:02, right when Sheridan and I got here. No time to move the body. I barely had time to stuff the trash bags in the dumpster before the cars filled the lot, sirens screaming. We didn't have time to move, or run, or even think up a story.

Sheridan comes up behind me. I know it's her from the soft vanilla-orange scent on the breeze. "I called my dad." She hugs her arms around herself. "He and Alpha Green are gonna pull strings, try to figure out an explanation for the bite marks on the body."

I give a short nod. I hate asking for favors, but the Phoenix pack has more clout with human officials than I'll ever have.

"We should also let Frangelico know." I rub the back of my neck. I'm getting a headache thinking about having that little conversation.

"Yeah, and Garrett should be here soon. He's bringing Amber." Sheridan chafes her arms. She shivering in her jacket—the one I gave her. I want to pull her into my arms, but don't think she'll allow it. At least she's wrapped up in something of mine.

We both watch the police tack up yellow tape over the door.

"That's it then." There's more bitterness in my tone that I mean. "I guess you got what you came for."

Her eyes widen. "What?"

"Fight Club's officially closed until further investigation. That's what you wanted, right? You and the Phoenix pack."

It's a mean shot, and one I definitely shouldn't be taking after marking her as my mate. The wolves have made and accepted their claim, but the wounds between our human sides...they haven't totally healed. And we still have a helluva lot to figure out.

"That isn't fair," she retorts, coldness in her tone. "You think I wanted this?"

Fuck.

"No," I sigh. I'm worn out and pissed, but it's not right to take it out on her. "I think it was just shit timing."

"I didn't want another body. I wanted to stop this from happening." She bites her lip, glancing back at the crime scene.

"Yeah." I deflate. The officials carted away the body, but in my mind's eye I'll always see the victim huddled at the door of the place I worked so hard to build.

"Hey," Garrett calls, crossing the lot with his mate, Amber, by his side. He stops in front of us, caressing his mate briefly as she points to Grizz and murmurs something. He nods and she rushes off, making a beeline for the grizzly standing a head taller than the officials buzzing angrily around him. Amber elbows her way into the fray, her voice rising about 'my client' this and 'jurisdiction' that.

"Thanks for coming." I grasp my alpha's hand and accept his back slap.

"Of course. We'll get through this."

Sheridan hovers just out of arm's reach.

"My dad knows?" Garrett asks.

"Yeah. Sheridan called him." We both wince.

"All right." He sighs. "I better brief him. Chin up. We'll figure this out."

"Yeah," I mutter. I know as well as he does that I put everyone's ass on the line. If word gets out about the marks on the victim's neck, all paranormals might be exposed. That would be a shit storm like we wouldn't believe.

Fuck me. How did this all go so wrong, so fast?

"Hey," Sheridan murmurs at my elbow. Even with just the few minutes we had to change and race over here, she looks pretty and perfect, not a hair out of place. Definitely doesn't belong in this shitty gravel lot, the site of a crime scene.

I did this. I brought her here, made this part of her life. Marked her, binding her forever to me. Dragging her down like I did before. Soon she'll wake up and realize she's sick of slumming. Only a matter of time.

"You okay?" She searches my face.

"Yeah." I can't bear to look at her anymore.

"Well"—she hesitates, then places a hand on my biceps. At her slight touch my dick gets hard—"I guess I better go."

I want to stop and drag her into my arms. Apologize for being an ass-wipe. But it's like high school all over again—her dad pointing out how I'm a bad influence on her. Now I've gone and marked her and we have so much shit to figure out. It's hard to see how we'll ever get through it.

I sigh. "Yeah, you better."

She sucks in a breath, like she didn't expect me to agree with her. I cradle her face and stroke her cheek. "You shouldn't have to see any of this ugliness."

Her expression softens. "I'm a big girl," she murmurs and squeezes my arm, but I don't look down at her, or watch her slowly take her leave.

My whole world is crashing down, and once more, she's here to witness it. If there ever was a reason we don't belong together, this is it.

CHAPTER ELEVEN

PRESENT

THE BLACK CAR is at it again, cruising slowly past my house while I watch through the blinds. I know it's Nero. Stupid vampire has a death wish.

He's going to find out I'm not a victim.

My phone rings with an unknown Tucson number. Could it be Trey? I've called him numerous times today, but he's only sent me short text replies saying he's up to his ears and will call me later.

"Hello?" I answer breathlessly.

"Sheridan."

My shoulders slump. "Dad."

Wait. I pull the phone away to check the screen again. "What are you doing with a Tucson number?"

"I'm in town on business. Pack business. Cleaning up the mess Garrett's wolves have made."

"Hey," I defend. "That had nothing to do with pack business. It was the vampires messing with them. Don't blame Garrett or his pack. They don't deserve it."

"So you say," my dad sniffs. "But we are all involved now. I'm actually calling because I am hearing disturbing rumors of your behavior."

"My behavior?" I get hot, then cold. *Stop it, Sheridan.* I'm a grown adult. I shouldn't be worried that I upset my daddy.

"Yes, Sheridan. Rumors that you've been hanging around with the Robson boy."

"He's not a boy, Dad. He's a man." A big man. "And I'm an adult wolf. I can hang around whomever I want."

"Not if you want to look responsible in the eyes of the pack."

"What does it matter how I look? I am responsible. Besides, it's not anyone's business."

"It is my business." My father pulls out his stern *sit and stay when I tell you* voice. "I am your father."

"Yes, but you don't tell me who to mate."

He sucks in a breath. "It's that serious then?"

"Maybe." Trey hasn't returned my calls all day, but my dad doesn't need to know that. "I thought you wanted grandpups."

"With a good, upstanding wolf from a respectable pack. Not a...a…"

"Son of a factory worker?"

My father growls instead of answering.

"Owner of a shifter fight club?" My anger simmers. It's

about time I called my dad on his obsession with pack hierarchy. "Or is it the fact that he's tattooed and owns a motorcycle that bothers you. 'Cause you know who had tats and rode a bike? Your own son, that's who." I bite back my words before I say something I can't take back. It's not my folks' fault my brother had a wild streak, that he died on his bike, doing what he loved.

"I know that," my dad snarls. "It's not any of those things. This Robson boy isn't good enough for you."

"Maybe not." I slump onto my desk, suddenly tired. Why am I defending someone who marked me, but still hasn't forgiven me? "He's a business owner and loyal pack member, who stuck out his neck to follow his dream. Isn't that worth something? Better than me, going to college and stepping into a position my dad pulled strings to get. It doesn't matter what degrees I have, being your daughter got me my job and gets me my promotions. I work hard, but if I wasn't a Green, I would have to work twice as hard to move up." Which is what Trey's done. "Maybe I should leave the brewery and get a starter position in another company. I might have to work the factory floor, but at least I'd know I earned it."

"You are not going to throw your education away," my dad snaps.

I shift on the desk and let the silence speak for me.

After a minute, my dad sighs. "Honey, you know I love you. I want what's best for you."

"I know." I realize I'm toying with the wisdom quote calendar. I haven't torn off the days in over a week. I knock it over instead. "Look, just let me do my job here? I'm doing my best. Do you trust me?"

When I finally get my dad off the phone, I shoot Trey a text. "Coming over tonight?" I wait for a minute, staring at the phone, but he doesn't text back. The bite on my shoulder aches and I rub it soothingly. *Relax, it's only been a minute. He's not mad at you. He just hasn't had a chance to see the phone.*

Gnawing my lip, I check out the window. The black car is gone. Which reminds me—someone should go to Toxic and formally tell Frangelico about what happened today. Even if his spics reported all the details, the pack should make contact, and because I've already visited Toxic, is should be me. Garrett's probably up to his eyeballs dealing with his dad. I shoot my cousin a quick text. By the time I've picked out an outfit—a practical black skirt and top that I could were to the U.N.—or a paranormal equivalent—Garrett's texted back a green light. "Sounds good. Bring backup."

Of course. Backup. I'll just call Trey. It's not like there's anything complicated going on between me and him.

My mating mark throbs as the phone rings and goes to voicemail. Voicemail? Seriously?

I hang up and set the phone down instead of chucking it across the room. There. Nice and professional. No need to get emotional. It's not like he's avoiding me.

I spend a good long time blowing out my hair. I'm about to start makeup when a chirp from my phone has me fumbling to see who it is. *Really, Sheridan? Desperate much?* It's an email from Garrett to the pack, informing us of a pack meeting. I'm bcc'd. Nice of him to include me. I forward it to my dad and let him know I'll be attending to represent the Phoenix pack. Business concluded.

Trey still hasn't texted. Should I try him again? Or give him a few more minutes to respond to my earlier attempts to contact him? I scroll through the day's texts, mine growing more and more worried, his more terse until finally, he's no longer answering.

That's when it hits me. I've been played. Trey played me. I can just hear him now, *I'm just going through a lot, babe. We need to take it slow. I'm not ready to settle down.* What was I thinking? Banging a guy whose idea of a business is selling beer on the sidelines of illegal fights in a run down warehouse? I'm smarter than this. I have my freaking MBA.

I slam my phone down and grab my mascara wand, opening my eyes wide and swiping aggressively. Trey thinks he can sleep with me and then just ghost? I mean, it's fine, it's not like he marked me...Oh, wait. He did. He marked me. Like I'm his mate. He freaking marked me like I'm his mate and less than twenty four hours later he won't even answer a freaking phone call when I need him.

Okay, calm down. I blink in the mirror, but my eyelashes stick together. Too much mascara. Never apply mascara while pissed. Too many layers makes eyelashes look like a sea urchin.

I'm being irrational. I know. But it's been an emotional day. And I don't like it when a guy promises to be with me forever by permanently scarring my skin, and then disappears. He gets a pass for having his new business and entire livelihood threatened. It's rough. But if I was really his mate, wouldn't he want to be with me?

I wash my face. I don't have time for this. I have a meeting with Frangelico.

I hope the vampires like lots of eyeshadow and mascara, because tonight I am full on grunge. I swap out my sophisticated skirt for a shorter one, and my sensible shoes for Doc Martens. At the last minute I pull on Trey's leather jacket because even though I am ready to run him over with my Mercedes, I still want to wrap myself in his scent. Stupid mating instinct.

The minute I enter the secret BDSM dungeon beneath the vampires' club Toxic that night, I know I've made a mistake. Leeches are everywhere, dressed in dark suits with their fangs on display. They ooze around, chaining their victims to walls, tying them to tables, stretching them on racks. The humans sigh and moan and slump in subspace. I want to shake them, scream at them to run. Get all the humans out and set the place on fire. *Love is not real and even if it is, you will not find it with freaking vampires! Yep, vampires are real and you're about to let one suck on you. Here, let me stake one and you can watch it burn.*

This grim thought sustains me as I weave around the scenes to find the king.

Eventually, I find him perched on a heavy wooden throne in the middle of room, overlooking a pair of quivering submissives splayed on crosses. They're being worked over by a large man in a black choker collar and leather harness, holding a violet wand.

An actual throne. Of course. I roll my eyes and march up to him, planting myself in front him. "We need to talk." I may have used up the last vestiges of my tact trying to reach Trey.

The king raises a brow but signals to his servant, who lowers the wand.

"Here? Or shall we step into my office?"

I want privacy, but don't really want to end up behind a closed door with a vampire. Lucius must see the struggle on my face, because he rises and claps his hands. "Let us walk together."

To my surprise, he comes down from the raised platform and falls in next to me. He doesn't offer me his arm, thank the fates, and doesn't seem to mind that I keep my distance, plus fall back a little to keep him in my sights. We're almost back to the front of the room, where some of the equipment has been moved to make room for a couch and two armchairs and a couple of small side tables, when I realize that I'm trailing behind him like a submissive.

Oh well. It's not like I actually am submissive to him. If he thinks I'm gonna obey him, he's got another think coming.

"What is this news?" Frangelico asks after we sit, and I decline his offer of a drink. I'm kinda proud I didn't shudder. What do vampires want their guests to drink? Bloody Marys?

Settling into my armchair, I tell him about the body found at the fight club and the human investigation: the whole messy business.

To his credit, Frangelico listens to my whole tale, not interrupting. He doesn't really change expression either. I bet he knows about the body—his spies are everywhere— but he plays along. Or maybe he is truly interested in how the werewolf pack is reacting to the whole mess. Plus the human angle—vampires are powerful, but they don't reproduce quickly. Which is why humans actually present a threat to everything paranormal. In the long run, both vamps and weres are outnumbered.

When I'm done, I bite my tongue through a few nervous beats of silence as he seems to ponder everything.

"So why do you come to me? This investigation, do you wish me to stop it?"

"No, no," I rush to say. "We'll take care of it. My alpha —Alpha Green—is already on it." I don't want to sic the vampires on law enforcement. "I just want the bodies— these victims with fang marks—to stop. Could it be one of your people, uh, going too far when they drink?"

"My people are too well-trained. Some of them chafe at my restrictions, but they would not dare break my rules." The king's voice turns frightening. "If they have, they will not like the consequences."

"Well." I wait until my stomach has returned to its normal position before continuing. "I'm not accusing anyone. But if it's not one from your nest, there's a rogue vampire. I can't imagine you'd be happy about that."

"No," Lucius practically hisses. "I would not."

"Hello, little wolf."

I crane my neck and Nero smirks down on me. "Oh hey."

The lieutenant glides around my chair to give his king a short bow. Frangelico acknowledges it by slightly raising his forefinger. His face seems more impassive. Is he happy about this interruption?

"Our guest tells me a body with our markings was found at the shifter fight club. Do you know anything about this?"

"Of course." Nero bows again. "I received reports

earlier and am monitoring the situation. When we have more intel, we can find the one who trespassed your laws."

"If it was one of mine, it would have been done on purpose," Lucius says with perfect calm, but all the hair on my body rises. "A deliberate mockery of the peace I have ordered between my people and the wolves."

Nero bows. When the king is upset, maybe it's best to hold your tongue. I fold my hands in my lap and keep watching the vampires, while avoiding eye contact. Nero is dressed in his usual suit and cowboy boots, although he's left off his jacket. His shirt sleeves are rolled up as if he just stepped out of a scene. He'd be hot, if he wasn't a leech.

"Perhaps we can find a way to strengthen the truce," Nero offers. I can't believe he spoke up with his king seething. He swivels to me, smooth as a door on a well-oiled hinge, and treats me to a shallow bow. Not that the courtesy works on me. "You've shown great willingness to deal with our nest. I'd love you to accompany me to an event our club is sponsoring downtown."

"What?" I ask dryly, pretending nonchalance at getting an invitation from a vampire. "Like a blood drive?"

Both Lucius and Nero laugh horribly.

"Your sense of humor is exquisite." Nero makes a show of wiping his eyes with a lace handkerchief. "Not a blood drive. A free nighttime concert by one of our more talented...ah...protégés."

I blink, not sure if I'm more disturbed that he has extended an invitation to me, or that Toxic is sponsoring a concert for humans, or that they have protégés. The event sounds like a trap for unsuspecting victims.

"I would be honored if you'd accompany me," Nero continues.

I tilt my head, trying to make sense of this. "What, like a date?" My brain is still scrambling to catch up.

"If you like."

"I'm not one of your victims," I growl. What does he think, he can wine and dine me and then convince me to come back for a scene so he can wine and dine on me?

"Of course not." His smile says otherwise. "It would be a simple experiment. We can prove that vampires and wolves can enjoy each other's company. We would be seen together as equals."

I press my lips together, trying to figure out the angle. Nero is obsessed with me. How will the pack take it if I step out with him? Will they see it as a play for peace, or a sign that I'm in thrall? How will Garrett and his pack see it?

More importantly, how will Trey?

"Let me get this straight. You invited me to a concert. You and I would go out together to see and be seen. And then what?"

"We would see where things lead." Nero sketches an eloquent gesture with his hands.

I shake my head. I'm getting a little muzzy. "Sounds like a date."

"It can be a date," Nero's voice mesmerizes me. "If you want it to be."

I'm about to answer when a shadow falls between us.

"Fuck no." A big guy barrels down on us from the

direction of the staircase. His scent slams into me a second before he comes into the light, every angle of his face tense and livid.

"Trey," I gasp as he inserts himself between me and the vampire in shirtsleeves. They're both tall, but Trey is bigger, bulkier, and madder than a wolf who's missed his prey.

Trey's scent swarms my senses and my head clears.

"What the fuck do you think you're doing, leech?" Trey growls.

"Making polite conversation with a lady. What's it to you, dog?"

"She's not going anywhere with you. She's mine."

I touch the place on my neck where he marked me, and warmth pours through me. A sense of rightness. My head clears even more.

The two glare at each other. Beyond them, Frangelico hasn't moved. He looks almost amused.

Nero looks smug. "My invitation wasn't to you, but to the lady."

"That's it," Trey snarls. "You're going down. I challenge you to a fight."

"Trey, what are you doing?" I whisper. At the sight of Trey, big and bold and present, all my earlier rage disappears. Crazy emotions are crazy.

"You, challenge a vampire?" Nero's laugh could curdle milk. "How amusing."

"One hour," Trey grits out. "At the arroyo."

"What," I gasp. "No. This is stupid—"

"Done," Nero spits. He disappears and reappears behind his king's seat.

"I do not allow my children to fight," Frangelico says. His face is blanker than usual. Maybe he's not happy at Nero's antics, either. "But he can sponsor a substitute."

"I won't fight one of your poor victims," Trey snaps.

"Oh, do not worry, wolf," Nero laughs. "My second will be a shifter. A fighter that is your equal. Or better."

~

Trey

I KNOW IT'S STUPID, but challenging that vampire and making him back down, hide behind his king? It felt good. Sucker has a death wish. Ever since he approached Sheridan at the club, I've been dying to stake him.

Fates, she was nearly under his spell. I had to do something before Nero stuck his fangs where they don't belong. Sheridan and I might be at odds, but she's mine.

"You were not invited here," Nero hisses at me.

I fold my arms over my chest. "I belong with Sheridan. Where she goes, I go. She's under my protection."

"Could've fooled me, dog."

I growl at him, and Sheridan grabs my arm. "Trey, no. It's not worth it."

I shake her off, ready to go after Nero. Leech won't be so smug when I have my teeth at his throat. Sure, he can appear and disappear at will, but eventually that little trick will tire him out, and when it does, I'll be ready.

"Trey, please." Sheridan touches my back. Her voice cracks a little. "Get me out of here. I want to go."

Fuck. I can't refuse her. "This isn't over." I point at Nero, who just laughs. Frangelico turns his ultra blank face towards his lieutenant and mouths something before disappearing.

"Fuck that's creepy," I say to the empty air where the king stood seconds before. "Come on, Sheridan." I put my arm around her shoulders and she slumps in relief. We hustle all the way up the stairs, out the club and to her car. She turns and leans against her door.

"You okay?" I ask, settling my hands on her hips.

"Yes. You?"

"Yep."

"Thank the fates." She touches my cheek as if checking for damage, then slaps me.

"What the fuck?" I bite back my chuckle because I can tell she's really mad. Plus, it's really cute when she's worried about me.

"What were you thinking? Leaving me all day without answering my calls? Then bursting into my meeting and challenging a vampire? Are you insane?"

I grit my teeth because I wanted to return all those texts and calls, especially the one asking me if I'd spend the night. But I couldn't. I'm not right for Sheridan. She'll figure it out if I distance myself. "I am protecting you."

"I can protect myself." She stamps her foot. "That's why my pack sent me. Remember?"

My amusement vanishes, replaced by that same sick feeling I've had since the call came in this morning about the body. "Oh, I haven't forgotten whose side you're on."

"Oh that's rich. This isn't about pack politics. I'm on your side, Trey. Trying to keep us all from getting killed by leeches. Of course, it's a little hard when you just volunteered."

"He put his hands on you. I couldn't allow that." I bite back the words *You belong to me.*

Her gaze narrows as if she heard them. "I had it under control. Lucius won't let him harm me."

I bare my teeth at hearing her call the leech by his first name. "You put a lot of trust in the vampire."

"He and I were the only sane ones in there." She shakes her head, eyes sparking. Damn, she's hot when she's mad. "How'd you know I was here, anyway?"

"Tracked your phone."

Her mouth drops open.

I shrug. "You can learn a few things outside of college, too."

"I don't question your intelligence," she protests. "At least, I didn't until you burst into Toxic and challenged a leech to a fight. What were you thinking?"

My wolf is still bristling and possessive, so I can't help but snap, "You saying I can't fight?"

She blows out a breath. "No, Trey. This isn't a male ego thing. Nero is dangerous."

I shrug. If Nero shows up, I'll have garlic and a stake ready.

"I can't believe this." Sheridan throws her hands up. "He could kill you!"

"I thought you said Lucius won't let him."

Sheridan growls.

"Sweetheart, I got it under control." Not really, but imagining ways to hurt the vampire will satisfy some of my wolf's bloodlust. "It's nice that you care."

"Whatever." Sheridan folds her arms under her boobs. Unfortunately, it just pushes them up higher. "The fight's not going to happen. There's no shifter who will agree to fight for a vampire."

"We'll see. I gotta go. Not gonna be late to my own challenge."

"Trey, this is just stupid!"

"It's my honor and it's over you." I mount my bike and face her. Whatever she sees in my expression makes her flinch. "Not stupid to me."

CHAPTER TWELVE

TWELVE YEARS AGO

BREAKING UP WITH SHERIDAN—HURTING her—makes me want to vomit. I shut myself in my room the next day, smoking weed and trying to forget.

My mom knocks a couple times, but I don't let her in.

She knows what this is. What I've done—for her.

It's not just for her, though. It's for Sheridan, too. I keep reminding myself that, every time her tear-bright eyes swim before my face. She may have sent the acceptance to Stanford in, but she didn't want to go.

I need to do this—not because her dad is an asshole, not because my mom's position in the pack is in danger, but because it's the right thing for Sheridan. She'll get over this hurt and make something of herself. She'll be stronger for it.

She texts me around four in the afternoon.

Sheridan: *Is this about Stanford??*

I tongue my lip ring, staring at the screen.

Fuck. She's too damn smart—she knows what I'm doing.

Fuck. Fuck. Fuck.

I need to seek out and stomp that part of me that's happy she knows. That's relieved that she still believes in me, that she understands I would never hurt her unless I had to.

If I let her believe I'm the good guy, she still won't leave. My mom will still be fucked.

I drag my ass out of bed. A new strategy forms in my head. The fact that it physically makes me ill tells me it's going to work.

Present

SHERIDAN

ONCE AGAIN I find myself clambering down the wall of the river basin in the middle of the night. The shifter equivalent of pistols at dawn.

I lose my footing and skid down the dry rocks.

"Need help?" I startle at the sudden voice at my elbow. Nero appears next to me.

"No," I snap. It was his stupid fault I'm here anyway,

scuffing the hell outta my Doc Martens. Well, his and Trey's.

Stupid male wolves. Gotta piss on everything to prove they own it.

"Not gonna piss on me," I mutter.

"Pardon?" The vampire oozes down the side of the arroyo, his snakeskin cowboy boots never seeming to touch the ground.

"Nothing." I reach the bottom of the basin and look around. There are a few humans down here, frat boy types standing around a fire they made in a metal trash can, laughing and passing around a bottle of cheap liquor. Vampire hangarounds. Facing them, silent, are Trey and Jared. Grizz is a huge shadow lurking behind them.

"Who needs the fight club when we have this?" Nero spreads his arms at the scene.

I stop and wrinkle my nose at the barren landscape, like an alien planet. The fight club has tons of charm compared to this.

"Well, leech," Trey shouts as Nero and I tromp towards him. "What's it gonna be? You ready to fight?"

Nero disappears from my side and reappears a few feet away, closer to Trey. I control my reaction, forcing my heartbeat to slow. I hate it when leeches do that. Not all of them can, but Lucius and his children seem to be particularly powerful.

"I will not be fighting. You heard my master." Is it my imagination, or did Nero grimace when he said the word *master*? Maybe the Frangelico Empire is headed for a coup.

"What am I doing here then? Wasting my time?" Trey

stretches his arms out in mockery of the vampire's previous gesture.

Don't bait the bloodsucker. It's not a quote from my wisdom calendar, but it should be. *Never mock a vampire.* Life advice by Dracula.

"No. I have someone for you to fight. Once you realize who, you may not be so eager."

"Like you can get a shifter to do your dirty work. Bring it on."

Nero clears his throat.

It takes me a moment to realize the fighter Nero refers to. When I do, my heart sinks.

Slowly, Grizz prowls around Trey and Jared and takes his place next to the vampire, facing them.

"No," I whisper.

"Sorry, boss." The grizzly rubs his scarred face, a tortured expression showing his conflict.

"Grizz?"

I can't see Trey's expression, but my heart cracks at the hopelessness in his voice.

"How long?" Jared snarls, stepping forward. Trey plants a hand on his friend's chest, holding him back from rushing the grizzly. "How long have you worked for the vampires?"

"Since before I met you." Grizz wraps his hands, not looking at anyone. Nero glances at him, smirking.

Trey shakes his head, and I feel sick by the hurt on his face. I know that look. He wore it the night Alpha Green threw them out for dealing pot and dishonoring the pack. The night I betrayed him.

"Trey." I hurry to his side, but he doesn't even look at me.

"Let's get this over with," Jared mutters and Grizz takes his place between the rocks. Jared rattles off a bunch of rules, including the out of bound areas, marked by larger stones.

Trey bows his head and flexes his fists. Grizz is a large, hulking mountain. I sense his regret, even though his scarred face just looks weary. What sort of hold do the vampires have on him, to get the loner grizzly under their control?

Jared finishes talking and backs out from in between the fighters. Nero and I stand opposite each other. The human hangarounds trickle over to the fight area, laughing and jeering until I growl at them.

Trey and Grizz ignore everyone but Jared, until he signals the fight to start. Then they focus on each other, so intent I expect electricity to crackle between them. Trey paces slowly around the edge of an imaginary circle. One of the humans throws a beer can. It hits the boundary rock with a crack like a shot. Neither Trey nor Grizz blink.

Please, please, let this be over soon. I fight to relax my shoulders and unclench my fists. Trey glances at me and for a moment I think he's gonna stop this madness and throw the fight.

Then he snaps into action and rushes Grizz, who roars loud enough to shake the ground. Fists lash out, Trey twisting at the last second to land a useless blow on the grizzly's massive arm. I swallow my heart, only to have it leap into my throat again when Grizz chases Trey, lumbering like the bear he is with incredible speed. Punches land with horrible thunks. I close my eyes a moment, but the smell of blood and the watchers' excitement are worse than watching the hits. I cover my ears instead.

The fighters exchange blow after blow. It's nothing like the graceful dance I witnessed when Trey fought before. This is raw and brutal, two apex predators doing their best to maim each other. Shifters can heal, yes, but when you break a bone, it can take a while, and it still hurts. It hurts bad.

"Enough," someone screams. I'm across the invisible boundary and between the fighters before I realize it's me; I'm the one who screamed. I turn to Trey, pleading. "Enough."

"Sheridan, get out of the way, baby." He motions to me. His face is cut and swollen. With as much damage as he's taken, his body will heal much slower.

"I can't. I can't watch this anymore. I can't let you do this!"

"Sweetheart," Trey whispers. "Please."

A movement behind me makes me whirl in time to see four hundred pounds of angry grizzly charging at me.

At the last second, I pivot and duck under his claws, set my shoulder into his abs and roll him off my back. He crashes into the dirt. The rocks around us rumble.

The bigger they are, the harder they fall.

The cheering cuts off like someone flipped a switch. The humans stare at me like they can't believe what I've done.

"That's enough," I repeat. "It's over. Everyone...go home."

A hiss, like steam escaping, slices the air. I whirl to face the vampire, and fight not to duck my head or tuck my tail. His face has transformed somehow, a monstrous caricature of something once human. Is this how vampires really look? "This isn't over, wolf," Nero says, and disappears.

Grizz rises slowly.

"You all right?" I ask him, but he ignores me. There's a nasty gash from a rock on the back of his head, already healing. He ignores that too.

"It wasn't personal," he tells Trey and Jared.

Trey frowns, and catches Jared's arm. Together they turn and walk back the way they came. The kids around the trashcan fire are already gone.

"Trey, wait," I shout. He waits. Jared looks back, shaking his head at both Grizz and me. He doesn't say anything, but I know what he and Trey are thinking.

Betrayed by one of their own. Again.

I reach out to touch the wounds on Trey's face, but he jerks back. "Trey, I'm sorry."

He shakes his head, weariness shadowing his face, making the bruises and cuts look even more disastrous. I can't believe he fought a grizzly bear.

"You shouldn't be messed up in any of this," he says. He doesn't sound like himself. He sounds ancient. Dead. He rubs his hand over his face. "You were getting glamoured by the vamp in there, and you're stepping in the middle of shifter fights in a fucking wash. You were born for so much better than this seedy life."

My eyes widen in alarm. What is he saying? This sounds like a freaking breakup. And he only marked me last night.

But I am sick of other people deciding what I was born for. I wasn't born to rule a pack. That job was for my brother. Or Garrett. Just because my father's pushed me into taking my brother's role, doesn't mean I belong in it. Yeah, I might do a damn good job, but that doesn't mean I want it.

I haven't been happy since—heck, since Trey and I split twelve years ago.

The first time he decided he knew better than me about what I should do with my life.

"You know what, Robson?" I snap.

My irritation catches Trey's attention, wakes him from his stupor. "What?" He's wary now, knows I have a bee in my bonnet.

"You don't get to choose for me. This is *my* life." I point at my chest. "It's not for you to decide what's safe for me, and what's dangerous. Or what I should be mixed up in, or *what college I go to.*"

He recoils at the mention of our first breakup. His skin pales under the moonlight, eyes grow haunted. "I'm sorry, Sheridan. I know I hurt you—I hurt us. But—" He stares over at "A" Mountain—the peak that bears the University of Arizona letter—and shakes his head. "I'd do it all over again. I'd do whatever it takes to make sure you live the life a wolf of your potential deserves."

Tears of fury spring into my eyes. I shove his chest and when he wheezes, I realize with horror, he probably has broken ribs. I stumble back from him. Can the two of us ever be together without hurting each other?

"You're not listening to me, Trey. You. Don't. Get. To choose for me. And until you figure that out, we have no future together."

"Yeah, well, maybe that's how it has to be." His bloody lips barely move.

Hot tears spill down my cheeks. I turn on my heel. "You're an idiot, Trey Robson!" I shout over my shoulder as I march off to my car.

CHAPTER THIRTEEN

TWELVE YEARS AGO

heridan

I'M TOO AGITATED to think. I have a mid-term to study for, but I spend the entire day Saturday thinking about Trey. I know what he's doing and I absolutely hate him for it.

Except I could never hate Trey, especially because I know he's doing this out of love.

For me.

Stupid, protective male wolves.

Even though I pick my phone up to text or call him every ten minutes, I vow to give it a little time. Let him play this out for a week or two. When he sees it's impossible for us to stay apart—when he's as broken and lonely as I am, he'll change his mind.

I'll promise to go to Stanford. Maybe I can get him to

come with me. I know he helps support his mom, but he could send her money from California.

Because I can't stand being cooped up in the house anymore, I head out to the mesa. My friends are there, texting me to come hang out with our classmates.

I drive up and park, but the moment I get there, my instincts scream.

Trey's motorcycle is parked with the other guys'. That shouldn't upset me. Not really.

But it does. I look around, trying to figure out what I'm aware of—why my wolf is snarling.

Pam, one of my best friends, jogs over to me, her face pinched. She grabs my arm. "Come on, we gotta get out of here." She tugs me back toward my car.

"Why?"

"I'll tell you later. Trust me, you don't want to be here."

I stop, the alarm bells ringing louder. "You have to tell me." My words are hard and firm. The alpha female in me coming out and dominating my softer friend.

She glances over her shoulder. "Did you and Trey break up?" She sounds scared, like I'm going to tear her throat out for asking.

I blink back the tears that pop in my eyes the moment she asks the question. "Yeah, sort of. Why?"

She jerks her head. "He's over there with Kaylee Ryder."

A snarl leaves my throat. I march off in the direction Pam indicated, and she follows right on my heels.

Sure enough. Trey is lounging on a picnic table—*our picnic table*—with his arm slung around Kaylee, his hand resting on her ass. He holds a beer in his hand, which he uses to gesture as he tells some apparently fascinating story.

Kaylee hangs on every word, laughing.

That *bi-atch.*

It's not a word I've ever even thought before, but right now, I'd like to tear a hole in Kaylee's flank, sink my teeth into her hind leg and show her who's the dominant wolf.

But that's not how things work. I'm in human form and the instinct for physical retribution must be resisted.

Oh fuck that.

I march forward and shove Trey's chest. I don't know what reaction I expect, but he doesn't move, nor does he look particularly surprised or upset to see me. His ice blue eyes watch me, unreadable.

I draw a fist back and clock him in the jaw. He grunts and rubs his face, still not offering me a single word, not a single reaction.

"Jerk-off," I mutter. "You'll regret this." I turn and stomp off as Pam gives him one more searing glare before following me.

When I get back home, all I can do is throw up. And when there's nothing left to heave, I flop onto my bed and plan his destruction.

Present

Trey

I'm COMPLETELY numb on the ride back to my apartment. I don't even remember getting here. All I know is I just made history repeat itself. I just broke Sheridan's heart again.

Or did she break mine?

I'm not even sure what happened back there.

How this day went so sideways.

I only know it's going to get worse when my phone rings and it's a Phoenix area code.

"Yeah?" I pull out my surliest tone. It's fucking past midnight. Whoever's calling, it's not going to be good.

I'm right.

An icy voice says, "Trey Robson? This is Mr. Green. Sheridan's father."

I take a deep breath. "What do you want?" I ask, even though I know. I had a conversation just like this with the asshole twelve years ago.

"I'm calling with a warning. Stay away from my daughter. You damn near ruined her life once, and I'll be damned if I allow it again."

"With all due respect," I say, even though he doesn't deserve anything, "Sheridan is a grown wolf. She makes her own decisions."

"That's why I'm calling. She doesn't want to contact you. I've spoken with her, and she's coming back home first thing."

I let my hand drop, the phone still squawking. Green goes on about shutting down the fight club, hunting down leeches and bringing the Tucson pack back in line, but after a minute, there's nothing but the ache in my chest, the rushing in my ears.

I fought so long, and so hard, and I'm right back to where I was: letting Sheridan Green go. Letting her ruin my life.

Rip out my heart.

Again.

SHERIDAN

I MOPE around the tiny casita, my body feeling twice as heavy and four times as lumbering as usual. It's because my wolf is on strike. She didn't want to get out of bed at all today.

I haven't taken anyone's calls—not my dad's, not my mom's, not Trey's. I listen to their voice messages, but they change nothing.

Trey apologized, but still won't own that my life is mine to choose. My dad is still insisting I get back up to Phoenix. And of course, he's recruited my mom toward that effort.

I grab a tissue and blow my nose, checking my face in the mirror. I look like hell. My eyes are red from crying and there are dark circles under them from lack of sleep.

I get a message from Alpha Green that he and my dad are planning to attend the Tucson pack meeting tonight, and he wants a full report before he gets there.

Well, tough shit. I'm not putting myself between the two packs any more. It was unwise of me to take this job in the first place, especially considering the history. But then, that's probably why I took it. I thought I was going to march in and show Trey what he missed out on, but really, I just wanted Trey. And I needed closure.

Now I have both but we're full circle again. Trey pushing me away, believing he's not good enough. Willing to damage us both in the name of protecting me.

Well, if he can't pull his head out of his ass, it's his loss. I'm not his clay to mold.

My wolf howls in protest, though. His mark throbs on my neck.

Screw it. I go to the closet and get dressed. I need to get out of this space before my wolf goes nuts.

I need to go back to the place Trey took me to run on the anniversary of Zach's death.

To heal in the desert.

∼

Trey

THE AIR at the fight club is old, stale. It's been only a day since the club was shut down.

Damn, this place is a dump. No wonder Sheridan hates it. A part of me is embarrassed she ever saw it, but it was her fault. I didn't ask her to come sniffing around me, waking up my wolf, bringing everything full circle. Try as I might, I don't hate her. I hate myself.

Gravel crunches outside and I tense until I scent Jared. My best friend tromps inside, ignoring the police tape.

"Hey," I greet him.

He stops and puts his hands in his pocket. "How long you gonna mope around like a pupper who lost his favorite stuffed animal?"

'What the fuck, man?" My fists clench. "I dare you to come closer and say that to my face."

Jared shrugs. "I would, but you're still looking a little beat up. What's wrong, man, not healing as fast?"

"You know it takes longer when there's internal damage. Fucker got my ribs." Didn't hurt as much as Grizz's betrayal.

"Yeah, about him. You want to sic the pack on him, make him pay?"

"Nah. Whatever the leeches got on him to make him theirs, it's worse punishment than we can ever dish out."

Jared shrugs again, as if he doesn't care either way. "And Sheridan? What you gonna do about her? Besides lie around and cry."

"Fuck you, man. I remember what you were like with Angelina."

"Yeah, and now I have a gorgeous mate and get laid every night. What's the deal, bro? This is the second time you've gotten torn up over this she-wolf." My friend cocks his head to the side, suddenly serious. "She's the one, isn't she?"

I blow out a breath. "Yeah. I... actually already marked her. But..."

"But what?"

I cast an impatient hand around the place. "What do I have to offer her? A shitstorm of no good, same as always."

Jared cocks a brow. "Don't you think you're selling her

a little short? Her parents may be snobby assholes, but Sheridan never was. You think she would've been slinging drinks here or prancing into vampire territory if she didn't love slumming it with you?"

I grimace at his choice of words and shrug.

"Dude. You have to go and get her."

"It's not that simple."

"It *is* that simple. You're a fucking wolf. You gave her your mark. That means she's yours. If she can't put up with you, chain her to your bed and give her orgasms until she changes her mind."

Jared's crude advice forces a reluctant smile from me.

My dick is fully on board with the plan.

Fully.

On board.

Tying Sheridan up would give me a chance to explore all the naughty costumes she has in her closet. Maybe I'd let her go only when she promised to model them for me. "Of course, she might kill me when my back is turned."

"That's what the orgasms are for, dumbass." Jared rolls his eyes. "Get her sweet, keep her sweet. Add a little playful punishment; before you know it, she's begging for your dick." My friend puts his arms behind his head with the smug smile of a man who's getting it and getting it often. "Then, you train her to give head."

Sheridan, tied and begging, opening her hot little mouth. Aww, fuck, now I'm hard as stone. "That's not a bad idea, actually."

"Told you I'm a genius."

"Wait," I sigh. "What about the pack?"

"What about it?"

"This is Sheridan. Everyone remembers what she did to us. Garrett hasn't even forgiven her, and she's his cousin."

"Garrett mated a human. Remember how we took it at first? Didn't exactly lay out the welcome mat." He shrugs. "The way I see it, you want this female, you claim her. Lay it out and make sure she has your back like you got hers. Things will work out with the pack."

"Think so?"

He shrugs again. "Anything is better than having you bum around like you're PMSing."

"Fuck you." I flip him off, but I do it with a smile.

"No, thanks, bro. That's Angelina's job," Jared smirks, and adds while I groan, "Pack meeting tonight at the club. Garrett wanted to make sure you knew. You haven't been answering your phone."

"It's off." I pull it out and wave it before powering it up. "Just needed some space."

"Yeah, I get it." Jared claps me on the back. "Welcome back to the land of the living."

"Thanks." I wave him out and square my shoulders. Now I just have to figure out how to fix this shit with Sheridan.

Once and for all.

CHAPTER FOURTEEN

TWELVE YEARS AGO

I SHOULD'VE EXPECTED it sooner, honestly. When I ride home from Garrett's and find Lance Green at my house, I realize I've been waiting for this moment since the first time I kissed his daughter.

He's sitting on our shabby couch, an untouched glass of water on the coffee table in front of him. My mom surges up from the armchair, a wild, frightened look in her eyes.

Who could blame her? Mr. Green is CFO of Wolf Ridge Brewery and sits at the very head of the pack after Emmett Green, Garrett's dad. My mom is the lowest of the pack—an omega. Which means keeping Lance happy is at the very top of her list, and I've fucked it up for her.

"Trey, honey," my mom chirps, twisting her hard-worked fingers together. "Mr. Green stopped by to see you."

I went still the moment I stepped in, but I force myself to incline my head in his direction now.

He walks toward me. "I'll have a word with you." He keeps going, right out the front door.

I follow him out, attempting a reassuring smile for my mom's benefit.

He walks down the steps and stands beside my motor-cycle, arms crossed. He's glaring at it, like it's the monster dating his daughter instead of me. Or like it's the bike that killed his son.

"She got into Stanford."

"Yes, sir, I know."

His head snaps up, fury blazing in his eyes. "She doesn't want to go." He speaks through clenched teeth. "Because of you, no doubt."

I work to swallow. "I made sure she sent in her accep-tance." I don't know why I said it—he's not going to find me to be the hero here by any stretch of the imagination.

He sneers like he doesn't believe me. "End it. You end things with her right now so she can go to college and focus on what's important—her education. I'm not going to let you screw up her whole goddamn life."

Despite the fact that he ranks way above me, my fingers curl into fists. Not at the insults to me, but because my wolf can't stand the threat to his claim. To the mating that hasn't yet been completed.

I somehow keep my upper lip from curling and showing my teeth. "I can't do that, Mr. Green."

In a flash, he tackles me to the ground, his hand around my throat. I hear my mom gasp from the doorway, and it's that sound that reminds me not to fight back. To surrender to his dominance.

"If you don't want me to throw you and your mom out of this pack, boy, you'll do what I tell you. *Break. It. Off.* You have one week."

I glare, but lift my chin to show my throat, which he still has in a choke hold. It's a sign of submission. One I have to offer.

He squeezes harder, cutting off my air. I refuse to struggle or show signs of stress—I just glare into his yellow eyes.

Fucker.

"I won't let you ruin her," he repeats, then abruptly releases me and gets up. He climbs in his car and drives away without another backward glance.

I walk inside and hold my mom, who's trembling and crying. "It's all right, Mom." I speak against her hair. "You don't need to worry about it. I already broke up with her."

Present

Sheridan

THE PACK CLUBHOUSE—AKA Garrett's nightclub Eclipse—is wall-to-wall stuffed with leather-clad wolves. I sneak in the back, ignoring ugly looks and burrowing deep into

Trey's jacket. I'd hoped the Tucson wolves had mostly forgiven me for what I'd done to them twelve years ago. Guess I was wrong.

"Why is she here?" one grumbles to his friends. Another shakes his head, looking straight at me, not bothering to hide his disgust. "Sad to see a wolf act like a rat."

Wolf Ridge basically shot itself in the foot kicking out Garrett, Trey and Jared, because nearly every young virile wolf in our generation and after followed them to Tucson. That's part of the reason I'm so high up in the pack—a female. Fifteen years ago it would've been unheard of. It should be Garrett poised to take the helm of Wolf Ridge Brewing, and of the pack.

I raise my chin and push to the front so I can see. My cousin Garrett stands on the stage, fingers hooked into his belt loops. Tank, the pack second, stands a little behind him to the right, massive arms folded across his chest. Neither look happy.

"Quiet down," Garrett says, and everyone settles. He doesn't shout, but he doesn't have to. His voice is infused with command. "We're here to talk about the events at the shifter fight club and the proposed treaty between us and the leeches."

"Burn 'em down," someone shouts, and a few more voices rumble approval.

"Shut up," Tank growls, and silence falls again.

Garrett continues, "The fact is, we had an agreement, and a few days later, they broke it."

"Not formally," Jared comments. He's right next to the platform, a boot propped on it. "We don't know which leech was behind the dead body."

"No, we don't," Garrett admits. "But we know it was a vampire. Whether or not Frangelico sanctioned the kill, it happened after the treaty, and on the premises of a shifter owned business. While we don't claim that part of town formally as our territory, Trey and Jared are our brothers. We have their back."

"Thanks, boss," Jared mutters.

Garrett nods. "Like it or not, we gotta do something." He glances at Tank, who steps forward and jerks his chin at the audience. "Floor's open," he announces. "Say your piece. Keep it civil or I'll throw you out."

Immediately, a rough looking wolf speaks up, "I say war. We take them out." A few rumbles of approval and Jared shakes his head.

"War means deaths and collateral damage. Last thing we want are vampires going after innocents."

"They already are," a dissenter points out, and everyone agrees.

Jared raises his voice, stepping onto the platform. "A few years ago I might be into fighting until death and glory. But now I have a mate. If there's a way to make this treaty work, I say we do it."

"But the vampires broke the treaty," the rough looking wolf says.

"Not Frangelico," I call out, pushing forward. "I met with him and I don't think he's behind it."

"Remind me how you're part of this, traitor?" someone mutters.

I whirl, teeth bared, but Garrett barks, "Sheridan, up here. Now."

Tucking my head a little, I obey. My cousin looks pissed.

"You met with Frangelico, right? What was his reaction?"

"He's not happy about this body, either." He seemed more unhappy about his orders being disobeyed than the actual death, but I leave that part out. "I think one of his lieutenants, might be acting without his permission. Just a gut feeling," I hasten to explain. "Nero has, um, a thing for me. He's been willing to stir up trouble." A glance around the room tells me the wolves don't believe me, and why should they? I'm an outsider who betrayed them once before. "Trey," I blurt before I can stop myself. Garrett raises a brow and I wish I could rewind and erase. Trey doesn't deserve to get dragged into this.

"What about Trey?" Garrett prods.

Darn. "Trey was with me. He can tell you more."

Garrett raises his voice. "Where's Trey?"

"Here," a rough voice makes my heart leap. Trey's tall form shoulders through the crowd. When he steps on the platform, the light hits his bruised face and a few shifters gasp.

"What happened?" Garrett growls.

"Had a little disagreement with a leech, so I fought him." Trey's expression is unrepentant.

"Got to be some real damage if it's still showing," Tank points out, and Trey shrugs.

"Let me get this straight," Garrett frowns. "You fought a vampire?"

"Not a vampire. One of his seconds. Frangelico doesn't

let his leeches fight. But what Sheridan says sounds about right." My heart quickens at Trey backing me up, only to realize he hasn't once looked at me. "I think one or a few of Frangelico's lieutenants are rogue."

"If that's the case, Frangelico should want to know who broke the treaty as much as we do," Tank says.

"Wolves and the leech king on the same side?" Garrett sounds doubtful, but shrugs.

More wolves start shouting out their opinions, and jostling each other. Someone pushes against me, and I push back, fighting to stay on my feet.

"Enough," Tank roars. Garrett holds up his hand for silence and gets it immediately.

"All right, discussion over. This isn't a democracy. We're a pack. I'm the leader, and if I see fit to deal with vampires, that's what we'll do. We stand our ground without a full out war. Keep looking for the killers, and hope Frangelico will do the same."

Even though they were about to riot a moment ago, the wolves around me nod agreement. I let myself relax.

That's when my dad and Alpha Green walk in.

My heart plummets.

They chose a back exit, so they come up behind the platform. Tank turns first, stepping off the platform to make way for Garrett's dad, the Wolf Ridge alpha. My alpha. Father and son face off, faces blank. They look so alike, only a few touches of gray signaling the elder.

Garrett speaks first. "Dad."

"Son," Alpha Green's voice is just a touch deeper than his eldest's. His stance is more wary, but he is the odd one out here. Most of the wolves present belong to Garrett. The split between the packs was mostly peaceful, but that could change.

Fates, I hope not. A war between packs would be worse than one with vampires.

"We're here because you're having a little trouble with the humans."

"It's a vampire problem, actually." Garrett steps closer to his dad and plants his feet. "But we're getting it under control."

Alpha Green raises a brow, just like his son does when he's skeptical. "I just spent the past twenty four hours meeting with contacts at the FBI and state police, calling in favors. They're labeling the body a drug overdose—elements of a toxic substance were found in the victim's blood stream. They also agreed to keep any curious details from the human media. For now."

The room seems to heave a relieved sigh. Garrett nods. "I appreciate your help. The whole shifter community does."

"I did what I had to do to protect our species," Alpha Green answers. "The question is, are you?"

Garrett bristles, but appears to gather patience. "We're dealing with the vampires. We have reason to believe this death was caused by a rogue leech. If we catch him, we can turn him over to Frangelico, end the deaths and keep the peace."

Alpha Green nods slowly.

"What about the fight club?" My dad clicks his teeth as if tasting the scent of prey. "It has been causing trouble for us since it opened. It is obviously a point of weakness for us wolves. First the authorities investigate the fights and the drug dealing, and now this body. Seems to me, we won't have much time to back you against the vampires if we're too busy hiding evidence from the humans. Cleaning up your mess."

"Well, son?" Alpha Green says to Garrett. "What do you intend to do about the fight club?"

"I can answer that," Trey calls out. All eyes turn to him, and he steps up on the platform, facing my dad, who visibly grimaces at the cuts and bruises all over Trey's face. "It was mostly my idea."

"Mine too," Jared puts in quickly, but Trey shakes his head.

"It was my idea to give the vampires free reign in the club. And I hired Grizz, too. He fought for us, and I thought he was solid. Now I realize we're caught up in something big here. Possibly a vampire coup. I don't want anything I've built to jeopardize my pack. I'm willing to pull the plug on it, if that's what my alpha thinks is best." He makes it obvious, he's looking at Garrett, not Alpha Green.

As Trey speaks, a smug look spreads over my father's face. My own hands clench into fists.

"Shut it down?" Garrett asks. "Is that what you want?"

Trey shrugs. Jared shakes his head, but mumbles something like, "Whatever you think is best."

Now my father is outright gloating. "It sounds like the best thing for the pack is shutting the fight club down. For good." A murmur goes around the room, rumblings of discontent. The fight club is popular. It's brought a lot of new wolves to town, new pack members. If Trey would just speak up, he'd find how many backers he has in the room. Instead, he folds his arms and stares out the window.

I want to run to Trey, and force him to look at me instead of my father. *Why won't you defend yourself?* I want to scream.

"Sounds like you have a clear course of action," Alpha Green says to his son. Garrett's eyes narrow, but he doesn't say anything. From what I know of my cousin, he's still thinking, and when he makes his decision, it could spell the end of Trey's dream. And for what? Because my dad used his political clout against my ex-boyfriend, and twisted everything to make it sound like Trey's fault.

It's not fair. But am I brave enough to stand against my pack, and, more importantly, my dad?

Being deeply loved by someone gives you strength, while loving someone deeply gives you courage. Not now, Lao Tzu.

I move closer to the platform. My dad catches my eye and I stop.

Life shrinks or expands in proportion to one's courage. — Anais Nin.

Great. I'm so scared my life is flashing before my eyes, and it consists entirely of cheesy wisdom quotes.

Trey steps down, and starts to walk away. It's now or never. I step onto the stage just as he's about to walk through the exit.

"Wait a minute," I hear myself say.

∽

Trey

I CAN'T BELIEVE IT. Sheridan steps up onto the platform, bold as you please. It's getting a little crowded, but she puts her hands on her hips in a proud Wonder Woman pose. "This isn't right, and you know it."

Her father bristles but Alpha Green raises his hand. "Say your piece."

"Frangelico decided to move here and claim territory. He's old, he's powerful, no one can stop him without lots of bloodshed. So far, we've had a peaceful treaty. Fight Club had nothing to do with the death, in fact, they were a target. We shouldn't be shutting it down. We should be defending it. Because we need a place like it. A place that's neutral where both vampire and shifter can interact. Someone saw the possibility of that, and decided to target it. And if you shut it down, you're playing right into their hands."

The room is silent. Alpha Green looks thoughtful, Sheridan's dad is incensed. But no one will speak until an alpha does.

Garrett steps up and claps a hand on Sheridan's shoulder. "She's right. When Fight Club was first set up, I was skeptical. But since it opened, we've had less pack violence, both between our members and with other animals. Any shifter with a grievance can go let out steam. And because it's not claimed by the pack, we're not responsible to arbitrate or reimburse any deaths."

Sheridan looks back at her cousin and he jerks his chin up in approval before dropping his hand.

"But it's not safe," Sheridan's dad says. "Any human could walk in there. The authorities are watching closely."

"So we move it. Or we fly under the radar for a few months. Human fights only. The concept remains. It's a good one." Garrett folds his arms over his chest, facing his father. "I don't like the vampires there any more than you do. But Frangelico isn't going anywhere. And he didn't come in and start a war right away. He seems to be willing to deal."

"Sheridan, I'm surprised at you," Sheridan's dad says. Sheridan flinches but doesn't cower. "I expected you to think more responsibly about things."

"Hey," Garrett intervenes. "You sent her to scope the situation. Either you trust her or you don't."

Garrett's dad's eyebrows go up, and the two stare at each other for a moment. Alpha Green breaks away first, not lowering his gaze. He looks almost proud. "It's up to you, son. It's your territory. Phoenix will back you."

"Fight Club stays open," Garrett commands. A shout of victory goes up. Someone claps me on the back.

"We're not done yet," Tank growls. "We need to solve the crime. Get it sorted with the vampires. Time is running out."

He and Garrett start giving out orders. Sheridan steps down, becomes one with the crowd. Probably hiding from her dad. I don't blame her. It took guts for her to stand up to her father.

She'll be leaving, and it's for the best. She deserves a good life, one I can't give her.

On that thought, I hit the exit. Time to get on my bike and ride, clear my head. If by the time I get back, Sheridan's gone, I'll know where I stand. At least I'll have the fight club to focus on. And Mr. Green's face, the moment his precious little girl grew up and called him on his shit.

"Robson," someone snarls behind me and I whirl.

Lance Green prowls up, his eyes shifter bright. "Stay away from my daughter."

I stare down at him. Why was I ever intimidated by this guy? I can just pack up my mom and have her move. She'll probably be better off in Tucson anyway, away from those snotty wolves.

Mr. Green growls, "If you try to keep her here, I will end you and your pathetic little club. Do you hear me?"

"No."

A vein practically leaps off his forehead. "What?"

"I said *no*. Listen, graybeard. Sheridan's an adult. She makes her own decisions. She made it pretty clear in there, but if you won't accept it, that's between you and her. I know you want to protect her, but if you think you threatening me is gonna work this time, you got another think coming."

"You can't talk to me this way, you mangy—"

"Shut it." I stab my finger into the older wolf's shoulder. He may have seniority, but I'm bigger and stronger and taller and completely done. "Sheridan makes her own decisions. I know she has a good life in Phoenix, and I'm not gonna push her to give it all up for me. But I'm done kowtowing to you. I rolled over once. I'm not going to do it again." I spin on my boot and stride to my bike.

"How dare you talk to me—"

I growl at him and he stops in his tracks a few feet away. "It's over. You want to fight it out, get on the schedule at the club. I fight most Fridays." I start my bike and the engine's roar rips the air between us. "And one more thing. I hear you threatened my mother again or go after her job at the brewery, I'll challenge you for dominance." He whitens at that. A dominance fight would upset the balance of the Phoenix pack, but I don't care. About time someone knocked him off his pedestal and put his shady dealings on display. "I don't care how many I have to fight to do it. I'm young and tough and I might just win." With that, I hit the gas and speed outta there, not bothering to look back.

GARRETT IS ABOUT to wrap up his alpha speech when I see my dad leave, following Trey. That can't mean anything good. I push my way to the exit, hurrying to the parking lot in time to hear Trey shouting my name.

"Sheridan makes her own decisions. I know she has a good life in Phoenix, and I'm not gonna push her to give it all up for me." He jabs his finger into my dad's chest again. "But I'm done kowtowing to you. I rolled over once. I'm not going to do it again."

What the heck? What does Trey mean? I bite my tongue, hugging the wall.

My father looks insulted, huffing and puffing something as Trey walks away, but Trey is having none of it.

"It's over. You want to fight it out, get on the schedule at the club. I fight most Fridays." Trey's bike cuts on. I jump from the shadows, ready to hustle over and get to the bottom of things, when Trey's shouted words stop me cold.

"And one more thing. I hear you threatened my mother again or go after her job at the brewery…" The rest of what he says is drowned out by the rushing in my ears.

My father threatened his mother. That's why Trey cheated. That's why he broke things off. That's why he's getting away again.

"Stop," I shout, but too late. Trey's gone, his bike growling up the road. He doesn't look back. I wouldn't, if I were him. What have we Greens ever given him but heartache? "No." I kick a rock against the wall. It's not satisfying enough. "Fuck," I spit. That's better.

"Sheridan." My dad turns, both stern and placating, ready with another lecture. I can see it on his face.

I am not in the mood. "What the *fucking fuck?*" I shriek at him.

He jerks back. "See here, young lady—"

"You threatened his mother?" Bootsteps at my back tell me we're no longer alone.

"Cuz?" Garrett's voice barely penetrates. I stalk forward, fists balled. I'm not going to hit my father, but he's about to get a piece of my mind.

"Sheridan—" my dad starts.

"I don't believe you. I got good grades and followed all

the rules, and what do you do? You go after my high school boyfriend? Not only that, but his family? What the fuck is wrong with you?"

My dad steps forward and I push him back. "Leave Trey alone. And his mother! You don't abuse your power in the pack to tell me who to date! You don't tell me who to date at all. Or *mate*, for that matter." I yank back my shirt collar to show Trey's mark.

"Sheridan," someone else says. Alpha Green. I should act submissive and listen to him, but I'm done acting. Real Sheridan is in the house and she is not hiding. I'm as alpha as the rest of them, if I want to be.

"I'm done. I hereby withdraw from the Wolf Ridge pack." As soon as I'm finished saying the words, I feel something crack inside me, like the pack bonds were hit by a hammer and shattered.

"Sheridan," my dad says, alarmed. "You can't—"

"You can't stop me," I snarl and stalk towards my Mercedes. Not quite the exit I wanted, driving off in a car my dad gave me, but whatever. I pay insurance and put gas in it; it's mine.

"Where will you go?" Alpha Green calls. I know he felt the backwash of the blow to my pack bonds.

"Anywhere but Wolf Ridge. Other than that, I don't know." Actually, I do know. I'm going to go pack my things, and call Trey and beg him to take me back. I'll hang out at the fight club. Sleep on the stoop if I have to. Well, there was just a dead body on the stoop, so maybe not that.

I throw the car into gear and peel out of there, and

don't look back. Garrett and his pack probably don't want me, but it doesn't matter.

Only Trey matters. I belong to him. Trey is my pack, and my home.

∽

Trey

I ROAR UP THE HIGHWAY, heading out of town. Fuck Tucson anyway.

Something tells me to pull over, so I do. There's no danger around, so I don't know what my wolf is telling me, but I pull out my phone and scroll through old messages. There are a bunch from Sheridan, most of them asking me to call back. I listen to each, trying to decipher the meaning behind her words. She sounds crisp and professional, not desperate or weepy. But that's Sheridan. She's not about to lose it over a guy. Maybe what we have was really just her reliving her youth, sowing wild oats.

She came out here to do a job, and the job is done. There's really nothing for her here, except me. But I don't count. I can't give her the life she's meant to live.

"Fuck," I mutter. I'm tempted to toss the phone, but some instinct stills my head. My wolf is hoping she'll call us or something.

I slump on my bike. I'd give anything to have her call. I can stop myself from claiming her, if I stay away long enough for her to leave, but if she calls and chooses me, I'm hers.

I've always been hers.

❧

SHERIDAN

THE FIRST THING I do when I get home is throw the damn quote calendar in the trash. Wisdom is nice and all, but it's time I went with my gut.

My next call is to Garrett. He answers on the first ring. "Cuz?"

"I'm requesting asylum with your pack."

"I figured this was coming." He sighs. The voices and commotion in the background fades. A door shuts and his voice comes in clearer. "How long?"

"I don't know. Just...give me a couple of days to get my stuff together. Your pack probably won't be happy with me staying. Not after I got them all kicked out of Phoenix." I took a deep breath. "Garrett, I'm so sorry about that... about betraying you and the others. I was just so scared someone was going to get into real trouble, get hurt all over stupid drugs but..." I pause, knowing this wasn't the first time I'd apologized, but it would be the first time I'd told the complete truth. "When Trey broke up with me, I thought I'd die, but then when he took up with Kaylee... something inside me broke... *I broke.* I just got so mad. I know that doesn't excuse what I did, but—"

"Maybe not," Garrett says slowly. "And I won't lie and say we weren't really hurt... we were. But maybe it wasn't just you. Maybe everything happened as it did because of the fates. If you hadn't betrayed us, we wouldn't have been kicked out of the pack. If we weren't banned, we wouldn't have come to Tucson and formed a new pack. Our own pack. Most of our members have good lives here. Better, one might argue, than the scraps they would've had to fight over in Phoenix. But that doesn't mean they'll forgive you as easily as I did. If you try to join my pack, they won't make it easy on ya."

"I know. I deserve it."

"Tell you what, kid. You got asylum as long as you need. As long as you're on our turf, no one messes with you. But to join our pack you need a sponsor."

"Sponsor?"

"Yeah. And there's only one who I trust to look out for you."

Trey. My heart leaps up, only to plummet. "He's not talking to me."

"You stood up to your father and mine tonight. Not to mention handling meets with the vampires. If Trey wants you in, I could use you."

"Thanks, Cuz." We end the call and I let the phone drop. Now I just need to find Trey and grovel. And for that I need the right outfit...

There's a strange scratching on the window, a figure moving in the shadows. I rip the curtain aside and glare at the creepy vampire beyond the glass.

"Nero." I knew it. Yep, there's his black car is parked at the curb.

"Hello, little wolf." He draws his nails down the window and I grit my teeth at the horrible sound. I close the curtain, and open my desk drawer, drawing out a little surprise I have ready.

When I open the door, Nero is waiting.

He pushes back the silky blond curtain of his hair, licking his lips. His fangs flash as he caresses the air between him and me, as if there's a solid wall keeping him from crossing the threshold. "Little wolf, little wolf, let me come in."

"Not by the hair of my chinny chin chin," I say, and have an idea. "But if you tell me who left the dead body at Fight Club, I'll come out to you."

Nero raises a brow. "Why do you wish to know?"

"I'm impressed," I lie. "Lucius is so old he's practically all powerful. Whoever dares to disobey him must be very strong."

"Oh I am, lady wolf. I will show you how strong."

I cock my head to the side. "So it was you?"

"Yes," he hisses.

"Why?"

"Frangelico is old, but he has forgotten his purpose. Vampires are made to rule. Me and my brethren, we keep the old ways."

"Brethren?" Dang, there were more of them flouting Lucius' rules. They hadn't done much yet, but they were probably only beginning.

"Soon you will know. The world will know." Nero licks his lips. Did I ever think he was hot? "Now come out, little wolf."

"Okay. But first"—I twitch aside my bathrobe sleeve, and raise the Glock I bought after I took out a frat boy

—"say hello to my little friend," I quote, and aim for the vampire's crotch.

Trey

THE CALL COMES in right as I'm about to pack up and ride back. Sheridan's number scrolls across the screen as if I've conjured it. In my rush to answer, I almost drop the phone.

"Trey?" Sheridan's voice wavers, just a little, and I'm on my feet, muscles tight and ready to fight.

"What's wrong, sweetheart?" If her father yelled at her, so help me...

"I have a...leech problem."

I kick up my bike's kickstand before she's gotten half her explanation out. "Where are you?"

"At the casita."

"Stay there. Stay put."

"I've got it mostly under control, I just—"

"Do as I say," I order, and roll out.

I break a speed record getting back to Sheridan's place. My motorcycle races through the old barrio, pulling in behind a black sedan that smells of vampire.

Sheridan's sitting on the stoop in a bathrobe, her eyes vacant.

I go to one knee. "You okay?"

"Yeah." She forces a smile.

"What happened?"

"I had a visitor." She nods to the dark car parked on the street in front of her house. "I shot him." Twitching aside a fold of her bathrobe, she uncovers a gun with an extended muzzle.

"Whoa." I hold out my hand. I want to know what the hell happened, but Sheridan's acting so weird, probably best to go slow. I pick the pistol up and examine it. It smells funny.

"And no one called the cops?" I glance around but all the houses are dark and silent. No one is squinting through the blinds at their neighbor in a bathrobe, which is good, because they'd also see a big scary biker carrying arms.

"I had a suppressor."

"I can't believe this."

She shrugs. "Speak softly and carry a big gun."

"All right. Where's the body?"

"Secured. It's Nero."

"You shot a vampire?" Come to think of it, the gun smells like garlic.

"And staked him halfway. It won't keep him down forever, but it'll buy us some time."

"For what?"

She rises and shakes her hair out of her pony tail. "I need to dress, and then I need an escort."

"Escort?" I blurt. This is all going too fast.

"Yeah." She pauses on the threshold. "He confessed to killing the fight club victim, so we need to deliver him to Frangelico."

Before she can disappear into the house, I catch her

hand. There's no time, but I have to say something. "Wait. Sheridan. You're really okay?"

"I was in shock a little. But now I'm fine. You're here." She pecks me on the lips. Again, she starts to go and I tug her back.

"There isn't time to discuss this now," I tell her. "But when you were in danger you called me."

"Yes."

"You chose me."

Her expression softens. "Yes."

I kiss her, and let her go. "Go change. Fast. We'll talk later."

She grins and disappears, my little vampire huntress.

CHAPTER FIFTEEN

PRESENT

WE PULL up to Club Toxic an hour before dawn. Frangelico approaches, wearing a tux and opera gloves. I would roll my eyes, but Sheridan is dressed to match, in a red dress that's all poofy and spreads out in a two-foot radius, rustling as she walks. I'm gonna pull off all the frilly shit later, see if the bodice can survive without it. Her tits look amazing.

I clear my throat as the king approaches, flanked by two burly guys. I swallow, wondering if Grizz is working here now that it's out he's on their payroll. I'll never admit how much it hurt to find out he was a traitor. My chest is tight just thinking about it. At least he's not here now.

Frangelico snaps his fingers and his guards stop in

their tracks, letting Frangelico close the distance between us alone.

"No lieutenants this time?" I ask casually.

Frangelico shows his fangs, either smiling or threatening me. Probably both. "You will find, wolf, that I am capable of defending myself."

"Not tonight," Sheridan declares. "We don't want a fight."

"Very well," Lucius bows to her. She curtsies in return, and I roll my eyes. Stupid leeches, always going for this old-fashioned bullshit. I can tell the vampire king is eating it up, though, and step closer to Sheridan.

Lucius makes a show about glancing at the horizon. "Perhaps we can be about our business then. Dawn is close."

"Yeah," I mutter under my breath. "Wouldn't want you to end up fried."

Sheridan elbows me in the side as she moves to her Mercedes.

"We have something of yours." Sheridan motions towards the trunk and waits for the vampire king to nod permission. Slowly, she pops it and steps away. Lucius takes two steps forward, angling his head. His face goes ultra blank when he sees what's inside.

"Ah. Yes, that does belong to me. Tell me, wolf, how does my child end up in your trunk with a wooden stake in his chest?"

"He was stalking me," Sheridan tells him. "He came to my house and tried to get in. Confessed to leaving the body on Fight Club's doorstep. Something about 'keeping the old ways' and showing the world what real vampires are like. He and his vampire 'brethren.'" She raises her index fingers and wiggles them at the word 'brethren.' Lucius' face turns scary as Sheridan continues. "Anyhoo, I shot him and staked him, but only halfway. I figured you'd want to deal with him yourself."

I hold my breath as Frangelico studies my girl, her car, and his fallen lieutenant. Now we see if he'll enforce his own rules.

The smile that breaks out on Lucius' face makes me shiver. "Why, thank you, my dear. It is so nice to meet a wolf who respects a treaty." He motions to his bodyguards and they lumber forward, dragging the unconscious vampire out of the trunk and behind the building. They don't bother to be gentle.

"Poor Nero. So passionate and promising. I will have to punish him. And get to the bottom of this little coup." Lucius touches his tongue to his fangs. He doesn't look upset at all.

"I'll let my alpha know the treaty still stands," I say, and tug Sheridan's arm. Time to go, before the vampire decides he is angry after all, and wants to punish more than just Nero.

Before she can turn and follow me, Lucius says, "I've always loved she-wolves."

I whirl with an insult ready, but Sheridan stops me with a hand on my chest. "I got this," she tells me sweetly.

She smiles at the vampire, showing her fangs. "Careful. While we do appreciate your willingness to liaise with us, we don't always like vampires, and we're not interested in playing victim. I wouldn't want you to end up with your head cut off because you looked at a she-wolf the wrong way."

I stiffen, ready to fight. Sheridan just insulted a vampire king with a not-so-subtle threat.

Lucius Frangelico tosses back his head and laughs. We watch the pale column of his throat work, frozen in horror. Vampire laughter is the scariest fucking thing I've ever heard.

"Lovely," the leech says, shaking his head with glee. "Just lovely. Go now before I decide to keep you."

~

Trey

INSTEAD OF DRIVING HOME, I head for Gates Pass and cruise up to a scenic overlook. Day breaks, and for a while we don't speak, just watch the light and color unfurl over the valley. Sheridan slips her hand into mine. Fuck, this could've all gone down so much worse. But for now, I have my lady within reach and another beautiful day on the horizon.

Her hand strokes my hair. I capture it and nip her fingers until she laughs.

"We did it," she sighs, her outrageous dress rustling around her.

"You did." I kiss her fingers. "*Liaise*? Let me guess— word of the day calendar?" Her smile is not only enough of an answer, it has my cock twitching.

Yeah, I want to tip her over the hood of the car and

fuck her, dress and all, but we've both been through a lot. First I want to watch the sunrise with my baby, get her soft and sweet. Then I can tie her to the bed and give her orgasms until she agrees to never leave me.

"Club will open soon," I comment. "Cops have no reason to keep it closed, now."

"Good. I have big plans for it."

My head is so caught up with whips and chains and what type of rope would be best on her soft wrists that I have to rewind her words until I hear them properly. Then I rewind them again. "Excuse me?"

She wrinkles her nose. "You heard me. The concept is good, but you have a long way to go in execution. Fight Club could be awesome and legit, if we just implement a few safeguards."

I lean back against my seat, stunned. "So you're staying?"

She blinks at me a few times. "Well, Garrett says I can only stay if you sponsor me." She bats her eyes at me. "So what do you say?"

I grin so wide my face hurts. "You sure?"

She shrugs. "I never fit in with the Wolf Ridge pack. Just did a good job of faking it." She crawls into my lap, big dress and all. My arms close around her like she was made to be here. "With you, I don't have to fake it."

"Damn right."

She chuckles. "You okay with me being here?"

"Oh yeah." My arms tighten around her. "Now I don't have to go with my other plan to get you to stay."

"What plan?"

"Not gonna tell you. I might need it later, if you change your mind."

"I've made my decision. I'm not going to change my mind."

"Well, then I want to surprise you later." I slide my hand over the gown's tight bodice. "But it involves that collar and leash and ball gag, if you must know."

She giggles. "Awesome." She cuddles closer, tucking her head under my chin.

"So you want to work for Fight Club?"

"I already am." She snuggles back into me and it takes me a moment to remember what we were talking about. "I'm going to take over the books and operations, but I can't stop serving behind the bar. At least, until I teach Luka to make change. You need me."

"Damn right," I murmur, liking the feel of her in my arms. "I think I'll like being your boss."

"Boss? No. I have a business and marketing degree and an MBA. I'll be your boss." She pushes up and meets my gaze fiercely.

"You serious?"

"Fuck yes," she replies and despite myself I grin.

"You're cute when you swear. Say it again."

"No." She settles back in my lap with a sigh.

"I bet I can get you to say it again," I promise darkly.

She chuckles. "I look forward to having you try."

Sheridan

THE LIGHT SLANTS across Trey's face, gilding his features. I sigh a happy sigh. I don't know what I'm more grateful to him for; helping me secure peace with the vampires, or getting me to stand up to my dad. Now I get sunrises and sunsets and all the hours in between with him. He's my reward.

"Can we stop by the club first? I need to take some measurements." When he blinks at me, I continue, "For the new layout I'm going to design. Don't worry, we won't implement all the changes at once. We'll start with little upgrades the clients will appreciate. First is a new parking lot—I'm calling contractors tomorrow."

"Fuck me," Trey groans.

"Oh, that's also on the agenda. If you're good, and no one's around, you can do me in the club, up against the chain link fence."

He freezes, then grips my breast, hard. "Is that a promise?"

"Work hard, play hard."

"Come on," he growls. "I want to see what sort of sexy get up you got on under this dress."

"Okay." I grin at him and put my hand on his thigh as he puts my car in gear. I can't resist, but I wait until he's about to turn back onto the road before leaning close to whisper in his ear, "I'm not wearing anything."

The End

THANK you for reading *Alpha's Bane*—we hope you loved it! If you did, please consider leaving a review—they help indie authors so much!

Want more? Grizz' story is next— find out what his secret is, and what the vampires have on him that made him betray his own kind. Make sure you're on Renee or Lee's newsletter so you get the word when ***Alpha's Secret*** releases.

AUTHOR'S NOTE

A huge thank you to the people who make this series possible: Aubrey Cara, the best beta reader on Earth, and Maggie Ryan, our fabulous editor!

Lee Savino Goddesses and Renee's Romper Roomies— you bring us such joy!

And of course everyone who's read and reviewed the series thus far. We appreciate you! Stay tuned for Grizz' story. We're not telling who his mate will be, but hint: you've met her before!

XOXO

Renee & Lee

ALPHA'S TEMPTATION (BAD BOY ALPHAS, BOOK 1)

Read now

MINE TO PROTECT. MINE TO PUNISH. *MINE*.

I'm a lone wolf, and I like it that way. Banished from my birth pack after a bloodbath, I never wanted a mate.

Then I meet Kylie. *My temptation.* We're trapped in an elevator together, and her panic almost makes her pass out in my arms. She's strong, but broken. And she's hiding something.

My wolf wants to claim her. But she's human, and her delicate flesh won't survive a wolf's mark.

I'm too dangerous. I should stay away. But when I discover she's the hacker who nearly took down my company, I demand she submit to my punishment. And she will.

Kylie belongs to me.

ALPHA'S DANGER (BAD BOY ALPHAS, BOOK 2)

"YOU BROKE THE RULES, LITTLE HUMAN. I OWN YOU NOW."

I am an alpha wolf, one of the youngest in the States. I can pick any she-wolf in the pack for a mate. So why am I sniffing around the sexy human attorney next door? The minute I catch Amber's sweet scent, my wolf wants to claim her.

Hanging around is a bad idea, but I don't play by the rules. Amber acts all prim and proper, but she has a secret, too. She may not want her psychic abilities, but they're a gift.

I should let her go, but the way she fights me only makes me want her more. When she learns what I am, there's no escape for her. She's in my world, whether she likes it or not. I need her to use her gifts to help recover my missing sister—and I won't take no for an answer.

She's mine now.

READ NOW

ALPHA'S PRIZE (BAD BOY ALPHAS, BOOK 3)

MY CAPTIVE. MY MATE. MY PRIZE.

I didn't order the capture of the beautiful American she-wolf. I didn't buy her from the traffickers. I didn't even plan to claim her. But no male shifter could have withstood the test of a full moon and a locked room with Sedona, naked and shackled to the bed.

I lost control, not only claiming her, but also marking her, and leaving her pregnant with my wolfpup. I won't keep her prisoner, as much as I'd like to. I allow her to escape to the safety of her brother's pack.

But once marked, no she-wolf is ever really free. I will follow her to the ends of the Earth, if I must.

Sedona belongs to me.

Read Now

ALPHA'S CHALLENGE (BAD BOY ALPHAS, BOOK 4)

HOW TO DATE A WEREWOLF:

#1 Never call him 'Good Doggie.'

I've got a problem. A big, hairy problem. An enforcer from the Werewolves Motorcycle Club broke into my house. He thinks I know the Werewolves' secret, and the pack sent him to guard me.

#2 During a full moon, be ready to get freaky

By the time he decides I'm no threat, it's too late. His wolf has claimed me for his mate.

Too bad we can't stand each other…

 # 3 Bad girls get eaten in the bedroom

...until instincts take over. Things get wild. Naked under the full moon, this wolfman has me howling for more.

4 Break ups are hairy

Not even a visit from the mob, my abusive ex, my crazy mother and a road trip across the state in a hippie VW bus can shake him.

#5 Beware the mating bite

Because there's no running from a wolf when he decides you're his mate.

Read Now

ALPHA'S OBSESSION (BAD BOY ALPHA'S BOOK 5)

A werewolf, an owl shifter, and a scientist walk into a bar...

Sam

I was born in a lab, fostered out to humans, then tortured in a cage. Fate allowed me to escape, and I know why.

To balance the scales of justice. Right the misdeeds of the harvesters.

Nothing matters but taking down the man who made me what I am: A monster driven by revenge, whatever the cost.

Then I meet Layne. She thinks I'm a hero.

But she doesn't understand—If I don't follow this darkness to its end, it will consume me.

Layne

I've spent my life in the lab, researching the cure for the disease that killed my mom. No late nights out, no dates, definitely no boyfriend.

Then Sam breaks into my lab, steals my research, and kidnaps me. He's damaged. Crazy. And definitely not human.

He and his friends are on a mission to stop the company that's been torturing shifters, and now I'm a part of it.

Sam promises to protect me. And when he touches me, I feel reborn. But he's hellbent on revenge. He won't give it up.

Not even for me.

Read Now

ALPHA'S DESIRE (BAD BOY ALPHA'S BOOK 6)

She's the one girl this player can't have. A human.

I'm dying to claim the redhead who lights up the club every Saturday night.

I want to pull her into the storeroom and make her scream, but it wouldn't be right.

She's too pure. Too fresh. Too passionate.

Too *human.*

When she learns my secret, my alpha orders me to wipe her memories.

But I won't do it.

Still, I'm not mate material—I can't mark her and bring her into the pack.

What in the hell am I going to do with her?

Read Now

ALPHA'S WAR (BAD BOY ALPHA'S BOOK 7)

I marked you. You belong to me.

Nash

I've survived suicide missions in war zones. Shifter prison labs. The worst torture imaginable. Nothing knocked me off my feet... until the beautiful lioness they threw in my cage. We shared one night before our captors ripped us apart.

Now I'm free, and my lion is going insane. He'll destroy me from the inside out if I don't find my mate.

I don't know who she is. I don't know where she lives. All I have is a video of her. But I'll die if I don't find her, and make her mine.

I'm coming for you, Denali.

Denali

They took me from my home, they killed my pride,

they locked me up and forced me to breed. They took everything from me and still I survived.

But one night with a lion shifter destroyed me. Nash took the one thing my captors couldn't touch—my heart.

Somehow I escaped, and live in fear that they will come for me. It's killing my lioness, but I've got to hide—even from Nash. I've got to protect the one thing I have left to lose.

Our cub.

Read Now

ALPHA'S MISSION (BAD BOY ALPHAS BOOK 8)

THE MONSTER WANTS HER. HE WON'T BE DENIED.

I've become a monster.

I hear blood moving in people's veins. Scent their emotions.

I want to feed. To hunt. To mate...

I'm no longer a human--my life is over.

I've left everyone I love. I've gone rogue from the CIA.

My only hope is my handler.

Annabel gray is tough enough to face my monster. If I lose control, she won't hesitate to take me out. But I'm not the only predator out there. Someone's hunting Annabel.

She needs my protection.

But if I don't get my animal under control,
I may be her biggest threat yet.

Read now: *Alpha's Mission*

ABOUT RENEE ROSE

USA TODAY BESTSELLING AUTHOR RENEE ROSE is a naughty wordsmith who writes kinky romance novels. Named Eroticon USA's Next Top Erotic Author in 2013, she has also won *The Romance Reviews* Best Historical Romance, and *Spanking Romance Reviews'* Best Historical, Best Erotic, Best Ageplay and favorite author. She's hit #1 on Amazon in the Erotic Paranormal, Western and Sci-fi categories. She also pens BDSM stories under the name Darling Adams.

Renee loves to connect with readers! Please visit her on:
Facebook | | Bookbub | Goodreads | Amazon | Instagram Blog | Twitter

KING OF DIAMONDS - A DARK MAFIA ROMANCE EXCERPT

Want more? Check out Renee Rose's steamy new mafia series, Vegas Underground....

I grab the vacuum and head back into the bedroom. When I finish, I hear male voices in the living room.

"Hope you can get some sleep, Nico. How long's it been?" one of the voices asked.

"Forty-eight hours. Fucking insomnia."

"G'luck, see you later." A door clicks shut.

My heart immediately beats a little faster with excitement or nerves. Yes—I'm a fool. Later, I would realize my mistake in not marching right out and introducing myself, but Marissa has me nervous about the Tacones and I freeze up. The cart stands out in the living room, though. I decide to go into the bathroom and clean everything I can without getting fresh supplies. Finally, I give up, square my shoulders and head out.

I arrive in the living room and pull out three folded

towels, four hand towels and four washcloths. Out of my peripheral vision, I watch the broad shoulders and back of another finely dressed man.

He glances over then does a double-take. His dark eyes rake over me, lingering on my legs and traveling up to my breasts, then face. *"Who the fuck are you?"*

I should've expected that response, but it startles me anyway. He sounds scary. Seriously scary, and he walks toward me like he means business. He's beautiful, with dark wavy hair, a stubbled square jaw and thick-lashed eyes that bore a hole right through me.

"Huh? Who. The fuck. Are you?"

I panic. Instead of answering him, I turn and walk swiftly to the bathroom, as if putting fresh towels in his bathroom will fix everything.

He stalks after me and follows me in. "What are you doing in here?" He knocks the towels out of my hands.

Stunned, I stare down at them scattered on the floor. "I'm...housekeeping," I offer lamely. Damn my idiotic fascination with the mafia. This is not the freaking *Sopranos*. This is a real-life, dangerous man wearing a gun in a holster under his armpit. I know, because I see it when he reaches for me.

He grips my upper arms. "Bullshit. No one who looks like"—his eyes travel up and down the length of my body again—*"you*—works in housekeeping."

I blink, not sure what that means. I'm pretty, I know that, but there's nothing special about me. I'm your girl-next-door blue-eyed blonde type, on the short and curvy side. Not like my cousin Corey, who is tall, slender, red-haired and drop-dead gorgeous, with the confidence to match.

There's something lewd in the way he looks at me that makes it sound like I'm standing there in nipple tassels and a G-string instead of my short, fitted maid's dress. I play dumb. "I'm new. I've only been here a couple weeks."

He sports dark circles under his eyes, and I remember what he told the other man. He suffers from insomnia. Hasn't slept in forty-eight hours.

"Are you bugging the place?" he demands.

"Wha—" I can't even answer. I just stare like an idiot.

He starts frisking me for a weapon. "Is this a con? What do they think—I'm going to fuck you? Who sent you?"

I attempt to answer, but his warm hands sliding all over me make me forget what I was going to say. *Why is he talking about fucking me?*

He stands up and gives me a tiny shake. "Who. Sent. You?" His dark eyes mesmerize. He smells of the casino— of whiskey and cash, and beneath it, his own simmering essence.

"No one...I mean, Marissa!" I exclaim her name like a secret password, but it only seems to irritate him further.

He reaches out and runs his fingers swiftly along the collar of my housekeeping dress, as if checking for some hidden wiretap. I'm pretty sure the guy's half out of his mind, maybe delirious with sleep deprivation. Maybe just nuts. I freeze, not wanting to set him off.

To my shock, he yanks down the zipper on the front of my dress, all the way to my waist.

If I were my cousin Corey, daughter of a mean FBI

agent, I'd knee him in the balls, gun or not. But I was raised not to make waves. To be a nice girl and do what authority tells me to do.

So, like a freaking idiot, I just stand there. A tiny mewl leaves my lips, but I don't dare move, don't protest. He yanks the form-fitting dress to my waist and jerks it down over my hips.

I wrest my arms free from the fabric to wrap them around myself.

Nico Tacone shoves me aside to get the dress out from under my feet. He picks it up and runs his hands all over it, still searching for the mythical wiretap while I shiver in my bra and panties.

I fold my arms across my breasts. "Look, I'm not wearing a wire or bugging the place," I breathe. "I was helping Marissa and then she got a call—"

"Save it," he barks. "You're too fucking perfect. What's the con? What the fuck are you doing in here?"

I'm confounded. Should I keep arguing the truth when it only pisses him off? I swallow. None of the words in my head seem like the right ones to say.

He reaches for my bra.

I bat at his hands, heart pumping like I just did two back-to-back spin classes. He ignores my feeble resistance. The bra is a front hook and he obviously excels at removing women's lingerie because it's off faster than the dress. My breasts spring out with a bounce, and he glares at them, as if I bared them just to tempt him. He examines the bra, then tosses it on the floor and stares at me. His eyes dip once more to my breasts and his expression grows even more furious. "Real tits," he mutters as if that's a punishable offense.

I try to step back but I bump into the toilet. "I'm not hiding anything. I'm just a maid. I got hired two weeks ago. You can call Samuel."

He steps closer. Tragically, the hardened menace on his handsome face only increases his attractiveness to me. I really am wired wrong. My body thrills at the nearness of him, pussy dampening. Or maybe it's the fact that he just stripped me practically naked while he stands there fully clothed. I think this is a fetish to some people. Apparently, I'm one of them. If I wasn't so scared, it would be uber hot.

He palms my backside, warm fingers sliding over the satiny fabric of my panties, but he's not groping me, he's still working efficiently, checking for bugs. He slides a thumb under the gusset, running the fabric through his fingers. My belly flutters.

Oh God. The back of his thumb brushes my dewy slit. I cringe in embarrassment. His head jerks up and he stares at me in surprise, nostrils flaring.

Then his brows slammed down as if it pisses him off I'm turned on, as if it's a trick.

That's when things really go to shit.

He pulls out his gun and points it at my head—actually pushes the cold hard muzzle against my brow. *"What. The fuck. Are you doing here?"*

Vegas Underground, Book One
   by Renee Rose

I WARNED YOU.

I told you not to set foot in my casino again. I told you to stay away. Because if I see those hips swinging around my suite, I'll pin you against the wall and take you hard. And once I make you mine, I'm not gonna set you free.

Because I'm king of the Vegas underground and I take what I want.

So run. Stay the hell away from my casino.

Or I'll tie you to my bed. Put you on your knees.

Break you.

Or else come to me, beautiful…

READ NOW

WANT FREE RENEE ROSE BOOKS?

Go to http://www.owned.gr8.com to sign up for Renee Rose's newsletter and receive a free copy of *Theirs to Protect, Owned by the Marine, Theirs to Punish, The Alpha's Punishment, Disobedience at the Dressmaker's* and *Her Billionaire Boss*. In addition to the free stories, you will also get special pricing, exclusive previews and news of new releases.

His Captive Mortal
Deathless Love
Deathless Discipline

The Winter Storm: An Ever After Chronicle

SCI-FI
Zandian Masters Series
His Human Slave
His Human Prisoner
Training His Human
His Human Rebel
His Human Vessel
His Mate and Master
Zandian Pet
Night of the Zandians
Bought by the Zandians

The Hand of Vengeance
Her Alien Masters

DARK MAFIA ROMANCE
King of Diamonds
The Russian, The Don's Daughter, Mob Mistress, The Bossman

CONTEMPORARY
Her Royal Master (Royally Mine)
The Russian
Black Light: Valentine Roulette
Theirs to Protect

Scoring with Santa
Owned by the Marine
Theirs to Punish
Punishing Portia
The Professor's Girl
Safe in his Arms
Saved
The Elusive "O"

REGENCY

The Westerfield Trilogy
Humbled
Pleasing the Colonel

WESTERN

His Little Lapis
The Devil of Whiskey Row
The Outlaw's Bride

MEDIEVAL

Mercenary
Medieval Discipline
Lords and Ladies
The Knight's Prisoner
Betrothed
Held for Ransom
The Knight's Seduction
The Conquered Brides (5 book box set)

RENAISSANCE

Renaissance Discipline

AGEPLAY

BDSM under the name Darling Adams

ABOUT LEE SAVINO

Lee Savino is a USA today bestselling author, mom and choco-holic.

Warning: Do not read her Berserker series, or you will be addicted to the huge, dominant warriors who will stop at nothing to claim their mates.

I repeat: Do. Not. Read. The Berserker Saga. Particularly not the thrilling excerpt below.

Download a free book from www.leesavino.com (don't read that, either. Too much hot sexy lovin').

EXCERPT: SOLD TO THE BERSERKERS

A MÉNAGE SHIFTER ROMANCE

By Lee Savino

The day my stepfather sold me to the Berserkers, I woke at dawn with him leering over me. "Get up." He made to kick me and I scrambled out of my sleep stupor to my feet.

"I need your help with a delivery."

I nodded and glanced at my sleeping mother and siblings. I didn't trust my stepfather around my three younger sisters, but if I was gone with him all day, they'd be safe. I'd taken to carrying a dirk myself. I did not dare kill him; we needed him for food and shelter, but if he attacked me again, I would fight.

My mother's second husband hated me, ever since the last time he'd tried to take me and I had fought back. My mother was gone to market, and when he tried to grab me, something in me snapped. I would not let him touch me again. I fought, kicking and scratching, and finally grabbing an iron pot and scalding him with heated water.

He bellowed and looked as if he wanted to hurt me, but kept his distance. When my mother returned he pretended like nothing was wrong, but his eyes followed me with hatred and cunning.

Out loud he called me ugly and mocking the scar that marred my neck since a wild dog attacked me when I was young. I ignored this and kept my distance. I'd heard the taunts about my hideous face since the wounds had healed into scars, a mass of silver tissue at my neck.

That morning, I wrapped a scarf over my hair and scarred neck and followed my stepfather, carrying his wares down the old road. At first I thought we were headed to the great market, but when we reached the fork in the road and he went an unfamiliar way, I hesitated. Something wasn't right.

"This way, cur." He'd taken to calling me "dog". He'd taunted me, saying the only sounds I could make were grunts like a beast, so I might as well be one. He was right. The attack had taken my voice by damaging my throat.

If I followed him into the forest and he tried to kill me, I wouldn't even be able to cry out.

"There's a rich man who asked for his wares delivered to his door." He marched on without a backward glance and I followed.

I had lived all my life in the kingdom of Alba, but when my father died and my mother remarried, we moved to my stepfather's village in the highlands, at the foot of the great, forbidding mountains. There were stories of evil that lived in the dark crevices of the heights, but I'd never believed them.

I knew enough monsters living in plain sight.

The longer we walked, the lower the sun sank in the sky, the more I knew my stepfather was trying to trick me, that there was no rich man waiting for these wares.

When the path curved, and my stepfather stepped out from behind a boulder to surprise me, I was half ready, but before I could reach for my dirk he struck me so hard I fell.

I woke tied to a tree.

The light was lower, heralding dusk. I struggled silently, frantic gasps escaping from my scarred throat. My stepfather stepped into view and I felt a second of relief at a familiar face, before remembering the evil this man had wrought on my body. Whatever he was planning, it would bode ill for me, and my younger sisters. If I didn't survive, they would eventually share the same fate as mine.

"You're awake," he said. "Just in time for the sale."

I strained but my bonds held fast. As my stepfather approached, I realized that the scarf that I wrapped around my neck to hide my scars had fallen, exposing them. Out of habit, I twitched my head to the side, tucking my bad side towards my shoulder.

My stepfather smirked.

"So ugly," he sneered. "I could never find a husband for you, but I found someone to take you. A group of warriors passing through who saw you, and want to slake their lust on your body. Who knows, if you please them, they may let you live. But I doubt you'll survive these men. They're foreigners, mercenaries, come to fight for the king. Berserkers. If you're lucky your death will be swift when they tear you apart."

I'd heard the tales of berserker warriors, fearsome warriors of old. Ageless, timeless, they'd sailed over the seas to the land, plundering, killing, taking slaves, they fought for our kings, and their own. Nothing could stand in their path when they went into a killing rage.

I fought to keep my fear off my face. Berserker's were a myth, so my stepfather had probably sold me to a band of passing soldiers who would take their pleasure from my flesh before leaving me for dead, or selling me on.

"I could've sold you long ago, if I stripped you bare and put a bag over you head to hide those scars."

His hands pawed at me, and I shied away from his disgusting breath. He slapped me, then tore at my braid, letting my hair spill over my face and shoulders.

Bound as I was, I still could glare at him. I could do nothing to stop the sale, but I hoped my fierce expression told him I'd fight to the death if he tried to force himself on me.

His hand started to wander down towards my breast when a shadow moved on the edge of the clearing. It caught my eye and I startled. My stepfather stepped back as the warriors poured from the trees.

My first thought was that they were not men, but beasts. They prowled forward, dark shapes almost one with the shadows. A few wore animal pelts and held back, lurking on the edge of the woods. Two came forward, wearing the garb of warriors, bristling with weapons. One had dark hair, and the other long, dirty blond with a beard to match.

Their eyes glowed with a terrifying light.

As they approached, the smell of raw meat and blood wafted over us, and my stomach twisted. I was glad my stepfather hadn't fed me all day, or I would've emptied my guts on the ground.

My stepfather's face and tone took on the wheedling expression I'd seen when he was selling in the market.

"Good evening, sirs," he cringed before the largest, the blond with hair streaming down his chest.

They were perfectly silent, but the blond approached, fixing me with strange golden eyes.

Their faces were fair enough, but their hulking forms and the quick, light way they moved made me catch my breath. I had never seen such massive men. Beside them, my stepfather looked like an ugly dwarf.

"This is the one you wanted," my stepfather continued. "She's healthy and strong. She will be a good slave for you."

My body would've shaken with terror, if I were not bound so tightly.

A dark haired warrior stepped up beside the blond and the two exchanged a look.

"You asked for the one with scars." My stepfather took my hair and jerked my head back, exposing the horrible, silvery mass. I shut my eyes, tears squeezing out at the sudden pain and humiliation.

The next thing I knew, my stepfather's grip loosened.

A grunt, and I opened my eyes to see the dark haired warrior standing at my side. My stepfather sprawled on the ground as if he'd been pushed.

The blond leader prodded a boot into my stepfather's side.

"Get up," the blond said, in a voice that was more a growl than a human sound. It curdled my blood. My stepfather scrambled to his feet.

The black haired man cut away the last of my bonds, and I sagged forward. I would've fallen but he caught me easily and set me on my feet, keeping his arms around me. I was not the smallest woman, but he was a giant. Muscles bulged in his arms and chest, but he held me carefully. I stared at him, taking in his raven dark hair and strange gold eyes.

He tucked me closer to his muscled body.

Meanwhile, my stepfather whined. "I just wanted to show you the scars—"

Again that frightening growl from the blond. "You don't touch what is ours."

"I don't want to touch her." My stepfather spat.

Despite myself, I cowered against the man who held me. A stranger I had never met, he was still a safer haven than my stepfather.

"I only wish to make sure you are satisfied, milords. Do you want to sample her?" my stepfather asked in an evil tone. He wanted to see me torn apart.

A growl rumbled under my ear and I lifted my head. Who were these men, these great warriors who had bought and paid for me? The arms around my body were strong and solid, inescapable, but the gold eyes looking down at me were kind. The warrior ran his thumb across the pad of my lips, and his fingers were gentle for such a large, violent looking warrior. Under the scent of blood, he smelled of snow and sharp cold, a clean scent.

He pressed his face against my head, breathing in a deep breath.

The blond was looking at us.

"It's her," the black haired man growled, his voice so guttural. "This is the one."

One of his hands came to cover the side of my face and throat, holding my face to his chest in a protective gesture.

I closed my eyes, relaxing in the solid warmth of the warrior's body.

A clink of gold, and the deed was done. I'd been sold.

Almost immediately, the warrior started pulling me away.

I fought my rising panic, wishing that my stepfather's was not the last familiar face I saw.

"Goodbye, Brenna," my stepfather smirked as the warriors streamed past him, following their blond leader into the forest.

"Wait," the blond stopped. Immediately the warriors grabbed my stepfather. "Her name is Brenna?"

"Yes. But you bought her. Call her what you like."

The dark haired warrior tugged me on. I half followed, half staggered along beside him. My nails bit into my palms so I could keep myself from panicking. Fighting the giant beside me wasn't an option. Neither was trying to outrun him.

The blond joined us, and the two warriors pulled me into the dark grove. Terrible thoughts poured into my mind. I belonged to these men, and now they would rape me, sate themselves with my body, then cut my throat and leave me for the wolves.

My eyes filled with tears, both angry and frightened.

They stopped as one and drew me between them. I shut my eyes in defiance, and the tears leaked out.

As I healed from the attack, I could make some noises, horrible, animal things, but they were so ugly, I stopped making any sounds at all. Sometimes, when alone, I'd sink into the river, open my mouth and try to scream. But no sound came out anymore. My throat had forgotten my voice.

Now the only sound in the grove was my harsh breathing.

I sensed the warriors on either side of me, their massive shapes towering over my fragile body. I was much smaller than them, tiny and petite beside their massive forms.

Right now I tried to remember to breathe and submit to these men. One blow and they could kill me.

My heart beat so hard it was painful. I was ready to die.

But when they touched me they were gentle. A hand brushed back my hair, then stroked my jaw. One steadied me from behind as the other cupped my head and turned my head this way and that. The one behind me gathered my hair behind me. I held my breath as the two massive warriors handled me.

I realized the smell of blood had fallen away, replaced by another scent, an animal musk that was much more pleasant.

A finger ran over my neck, near the scar and I sucked in a breath. The hands dropped away.

Their faces dipped close to mine, and I felt their breath on my skin as if they took deep scents of my hair.

"So good," one of them groaned.

I didn't understand. I was afraid of them taking me but I didn't know why they weren't.

"It's working," one murmured to the other. "The witch was right."

As they dipped their heads and scented me, my heart beat faster in response to their proximity. Something stirred deep inside me. Desire. A few minutes alone with these men and I'd been more intimate with them than any other.

As one they bent their heads to mine, nuzzling close to my neck a tingling spread over my skin.

I felt it then, unbidden, a stirring in my loins. Ever since I had come into womanhood, my desires were strong. Every month I fought the pull to find a man and join with him. I was hideous and destined to be an outcast and alone. But each full moon my body came alive, beset by waves of roiling lust until I felt desperate enough to grab the nearest man and beg him to give me sons.

The heat poured over me until I heard a gasp—one of the warriors jerked back and stepped away.

"She's ready," one growled. Instead of frightening, the sound excited me.

What was happening?

"Not here, brother," the blond rasped.

Without answering, the dark-haired one pulled me on.

For a while we walked, pushing through the forest and forded a stream. The heat in me faded as I followed, weak with hunger and fear, eventually stumbling on exhaustion numbed feet.

The dark-haired warrior stopped, and I flinched, expecting him to bully me into continuing on.

Instead, he guided me to face him. Again his hands came to me, stroking back my hair. I winced when I realized what he was doing: looking at my scar.

Involuntarily my head jerked and he let my chin go, offering me water instead. He held the skin while I drank, and when I'd had my fill he offered me dried meat, feeding me from his hand. I stared into the strange golden eyes, unable to keep the questions off my face: Who are you? What are you going to do with me?

When I was done, he lay a hand on his chest and uttered a guttural sound I didn't understand. He repeated it twice, then lay his hand on my chest.

"Brenna." I could barely make out my name, but I nodded.

A shadow of a smile curved his full lips. Shrugging off the gray pelt he wore, he wrapped it around my shoulders before pulling me back into the circle of his strong arms.

My heart beat faster. The pelt's warmth seeped into my tired body, and the big man held me steady. I still felt frightened, but waited obediently in the dark haired warrior's embrace. I dared not struggle.

The brush around us rippled and the warriors surrounded us. I shrank towards my black-haired captor, but he held me fast, turning me so I faced the warrior who seemed to be their leader.

The blond was so huge, my neck had to tip back to see him. He moved forward and I couldn't help trembling so hard I would've fallen if the dark haired warrior let me go. Every instinct in me screamed that this was a wild man, a beast a dangerous monster and I needed to run.

He reached out and I flinched.

His hand halted.

He swallowed, as if trying to remember how to use his voice.

"Brenna." My name was no more than a soft growl. "We mean you no harm."

I studied him. As big as the warriors were, the blond was one of the largest. He walked lightly, muscles bulging. Long locks of blond hair brushed his broad shoulders. His face was rawboned and half covered in a beard, the defining feature his great gold eyebrows over those amazing eyes.

When his gaze caught mine, his eyes glowed.

His hands touched my face, a thumb stroking my lips. He tilted it to and fro. He pushed my hair away from my neck. I shut my eyes, knowing what he saw, the white weals and gnarled tissue, healed into a disfiguring scar that had taken my voice, and nearly taken my life.

I barely remembered the attack: a large dark shape rushing at me from the shadows, then pain. Lots of pain.

My mother told me I lay near death for days. No one thought I would survive, but I did.

Some believed it would be better if I hadn't. Even though I healed from the attack, the scars marked my face and my life. The boys used to chase me down the street, throwing things. I grew up learning to blend into the shadows. To move silently so I wouldn't draw attention to myself. Later, when my mother married my stepfather, I learned to cower and hide.

Her body is pretty enough, my stepfather had said. *Just put a bag over her head so you can stand it.*

Now my new owner tipped my head this way and that, studying the scar. He nodded, looking satisfied. "The mark of the wolf," he rasped.

A ripple went around the assembled men, and the other warriors pressed closer. The black haired man held me still, hefty arms around my body.

I wished I could ask what the blond warrior meant.

The men surrounded me, staring at my hideous scars.

My blond captor released my jaw and I ducked my head down again in shame. His large, rough hands caught my head again, and raised it, but this time he cupped my face.

I shut my eyes. I couldn't even cry out. This man now owned me. I'd resigned myself to living life with a disfigured face, unwanted and unloved, but I'd never thought I'd become a slave.

"Brenna," The command came in that rasping growl. "Look at me."

Somehow I obeyed and met the leader's steady gaze.

Something in that golden glow mesmerized me, and I felt calmer.

"Do not be afraid." His throat worked for a moment, as if he was trying to remember how to speak. "Is it true you cannot speak?"

I nodded.

"Can you read or write?"

I shook my head. This was the strangest conversation I'd had in my nineteen years.

He looked frustrated, exchanging glances with the warrior who held me.

A voice spoke at my ear, still rough and guttural, but a bit more clearly than before. "We would like to find a way to talk to ye." The speaker turned me to face him, and I flinched as he brought his hand up, but he only examined the scars as the blond had.

By the time he was done, all warriors but the blond had melted away. Dark hair touched my cheek and I winced, realizing there was a bruise on my face from when my stepfather struck me.

The blond crowded closer, a sound rumbling in his great chest, not unlike a growl.

"Brenna," he said. "We will not hurt you. I swear it. No one will ever hurt you again."

The dark haired one took a few locks of my hair in his hand, gripping them lightly and raising them to his face. He breathed in my scent, then looked at me with glowing eyes and said in a clear voice.

"Ye belong to us now."

❧

The rest of the night passed in a blur. We walked into the woods, the thick darkness, and went along a path. The warriors went behind and before, I was safe in the middle.

Finally exhaustion took over and I stumbled. Instantly, the dark haired warrior swung me up in his arms, and the group's pace increased. His hand came up, pressing my face to his neck.

I must have slept, for when I woke again, the blond was carrying me. I lifted my head blinking in the starlight and cold night air. The warriors must have walked all night, and were still hiking, following a trail up a mountain. I roused a little and stared into the leaders golden eyes.

"Sleep," he grunted. "Almost home."

I do not know how long I slept, but as I slept I dreamed. The starlight fell away into a deeper darkness. I was in a warm, safe place with two warriors leaning over me, large hands sifting through my hair. One of them pulled out a dirk and sliced away my gown, and then the hands began stroking down my body. Their touches fed my heated desire, and in my dream I longed to pull their bodies over mine, wordlessly begging them to fill me.

Instead, I lay still as they touched me with reverent fingers. I heard them speak, but not out loud. They didn't use words but somehow I understood them.

"The witch was right. She calms the wolf."

A grunt of agreement, then a pause. "I can smell her heat."

"Patience, brother. We have waited this long."

They lay on either side of me, still touching me. In the darkness their eyes glowed.

"Brother," one said in a tone of awe. "The beast rests."

"As does mine."

"It has been so long."

"Too long. But the struggle is over. The beast will sleep again."

SOLD TO THE BERSERKERS

When Brenna's father sells her to a band of passing warriors, her only thought is to survive. She doesn't expect to be claimed by the two fearsome warriors who lead the Berserker clan. Kept in captivity, she is coddled and cared for, treated more like a savior than a slave. Can captivity lead to love? And when she discovers the truth behind the myth of the fearsome warriors, can she accept her place as the Berserkers' true mate?

Author's Note: *Sold to the Berserkers is a standalone, short, MFM ménage romance starring two huge, dominant warriors who make it all about the woman. Read the whole best-selling Berserker saga to see what readers are raving about...*

The Berserker Saga
Sold to the Berserkers

Mated to the Berserkers

Bred by the Berserkers (free novella available on leesavino.com)

Taken by the Berserkers

Given to the Berserkers

Claimed by the Berserkers

Rescued by the Berserkers - free on all sites, including Wattpad

Captured by the Berserkers

Kidnapped by the Berserkers

Bonded to the Berserkers

Berserker Babies

Owned by the Berserkers

Night of the Berserkers

Printed in Great Britain
by Amazon